SABRE WINGMAN

By

Thomas Willard

Approximately 32,500 words.

Contents

INTRODUCTION

Beginning in July 1944, shocked Allied bomber and photo-reconnaissance crews returning from missions over Germany started asking, “What was that thing, and where is ours?” The “thing” they were referring to was the Messerschmitt ME262, the first and only jet-powered fighter to see significant combat during World War II.

The new German jet fighters were 100 mph faster than the piston engine-propeller-driven P-51 escort fighters. As a result, the jets easily broke through the fighter screens to reach the bombers and were too swift for the bombers’ gunners to train their guns on, leaving the bombers essentially defenseless.

On 3 September 1944, USAAF Lieutenant General Carl Spaatz, commander of Allied Air Forces in Europe, wrote a letter to USAAF Commanding General Henry Arnold. In the letter, he expressed his fear that if enough enemy jets appeared over German targets, they could regain air supremacy over Germany and inflict sufficient losses to force the suspension of the Allied daylight bombing campaign.

Fortunately, the ME262s proved unreliable, too few in number, and arrived too late: Allied bombing had left the Luftwaffe little fuel for flying.

USAF pilots quickly developed tactics to exploit the jet fighter's weaknesses. For example, they used the "coyote-deer herding technique," with a pair of fighters bracketing a jet in a dog fight, with one P-51 running the jet to get him to turn and the other cutting in for an intercept-kill. And they loitered around German airfields, attacking the jets when they were most vulnerable, during takeoff and landing. The combination of these two tactics alone resulted in the loss of as many as two hundred and forty ME262s.

In fact, the Allies were about to deploy squadrons of their own jet fighters: the British, deploying their new Gloster Meteor, first flown in March 1943, and entering service in July 1944; and the US, fielding their new Lockheed P-80 Shooting Star, first flown in January 1944, and entering service in January 1945. Both planes used a version of the British-developed, Frank Whittle-designed centrifugal compressor jet engine. Unfortunately, neither fighter arrived in time to engage the German jet fighters in aerial combat, but their existence alone had a positive psychological effect on Allied aircrews.

Though the German jet fighters had no appreciable effect on the outcome of the war, their arrival did have significant consequences, signaling to military planners the world over the end of the era of propeller-driven fighters.

CHAPTER 1 – INVENTION OF THE TURBOJET ENGINE AND ITS DEVELOPMENT INTO THE GENERAL ELECTRIC J47

THE WRIGHT BROTHERS AND THE DEVELOPMENT OF THE AERO PROPELLER

Aviation historians credit the Wright brothers with being the first to achieve powered flight, having developed a system to control an aircraft's pitch, yaw, and roll. But just as significant a contribution was their 1902 insights leading to the twisted-airfoil design of the aero propeller.

Their reduced-scaled airfoil wind tunnel tests of wings showed that an airfoil's performance chiefly depends on its angle of attack (AOA): the angle between the chord of the airfoil and the oncoming airstream. And any airfoil shape has a maximum angle of attack that produces peak efficiency, above which the airfoil stalls and its lift quickly drops to zero.

The insights gained from these tests led them to be the first to realize that the optimum shape for an aircraft propeller was not the marine screw design their literature research had suggested but an airfoil. The propeller's airfoil would act like a wing, except producing a lift force, known as thrust with a propeller, in the forward instead of vertical direction.

Unlike a wing, though, whose angle of attack only varies with aircraft attitude, or pitch, a propeller's angle of attack varies with: the blade's pitch; the rotational speed, or engine rpm times the radius, which increases along the length of the propeller blade; and the forward airspeed.

Their findings showed that: an increase in engine rpm increases the angle of attack while an increase in airspeed reduces it; and that the ratio of airspeed to engine rpm - what later became known as the "advance ratio" - is a critical parameter in calculating the performance of a given propeller design in flight. They also realized that by incorporating a hub-to-tip twist in the blade, they could achieve a uniform angle of attack along the length of the propeller.

Orville Wright described the propeller design problem the brothers faced best in a 13 December 1930 article in *Flying Magazine*. He wrote,

"*It's hard to find even a point from which to make a start, for nothing about a propeller, or the medium in which it acts, stands still for a moment. The thrust depends upon the speed and the angle at which the blade strikes the air; the angle at which the blade strikes the air depends upon the speed at which the propeller is turning, the speed the machine is traveling forward, and the speed that the air is slipping backward; the slip of the air backward depends upon the thrust exerted by the propeller, and the amount of air acted upon. When any of these changes, it changes all the rest, as they are all interdependent upon one another.*"

This research was pretty impressive for a pair of bicycle mechanics from Dayton, Ohio, with no formal engineering education. But, in reality, they were a pair of brilliant experimentalists that outperformed the day's scientific elite in using the modern scientific method and set an example for later aviation pioneers to follow, like William Durand, Sanford Moss, and Frank Whittle.

In a series of full-scale propeller performance tests done from 1916 to 1924 at Stanford University for the US National Advisory Committee for Aeronautics (NACA), William F. Durand, Jr. - who would later chair the secret US government's committee responsible for the development of jet engines - extended the scope of the Wright brothers' propeller research.

The tests verified the accuracy of the Wright's results and conclusions – proving they were accurate to within one percent – and extended their range from the Wright's airspeed of 30 mph to 150 mph and altitude of 1100 feet to 3500 feet.

These tests helped establish the equations of propeller performance based on airfoil theory. In addition, they provided measured performance data for one hundred twenty-five NACA propeller numbered designs, used to design propellers for most US military and commercial aircraft from the 1920s through the 1950s.

Notably, the test results suggested that two upper limits restrict the speed of propeller-driven aircraft: approaching the speed of sound at the propeller's tip, resulting in a shock wave, with increased drag and loss of thrust; and attaining a forward airspeed where the propeller's angle of attack approaches zero, resulting in zero-thrust. Both conditions would occur at an airspeed of approximately 480 mph, seemingly restricting propeller-driven aircraft to that speed.

However, when the world's aircraft speed record was just 220 mph, few were concerned with this theoretical speed limit. It wasn't until the late 1920s, after significant improvements in aircraft engine and airframe design and with aircraft racer speeds approaching 300 mph, that visionary aircraft designers began looking for alternatives to the piston engine-driven propeller to power aircraft.

#

FRANK WHITTLE AND THE INVENTION OF THE TURBOJET ENGINE

In October 1929, Frank Whittle, a 22-year-old Royal Air Force (RAF) flight instructor trainee at RAF Upavon Aerodrome, Wiltshire, UK, presented an idea to the British Air Ministry that he'd been working on for the past two years while as an air cadet.

He proposed using a gas turbine to produce a jet exhaust instead of a propeller to power an aircraft - a turbojet engine.

While attending the RAF College at Cranwell in 1928, Whittle had written a thesis titled "Future Developments in Aircraft Design" to meet that term's thesis requirement. In his thesis, he suggested using a hybrid piston engine-gas turbine design to power aircraft and designing airplanes to fly at high-altitude where the drag would be less, predicting a maximum airspeed of over 600 mph.

For the next 18 months, working on his own, he continued to refine his idea, eventually arriving at the elegant, simplified solution he presented to the Air Ministry: a compressor-turbine combination, spinning on a common shaft, producing a jet exhaust to propel an aircraft.

Since his proposed design used a two-stage axial flow compressor feeding a single-sided centrifugal compressor, the Air Ministry asked the then-leading expert on axial flow compressors, Dr. Alan A. Griffith, to evaluate Whittle's design. Griffith, a research scientist at the Royal Aircraft Establishment (RAE), had just written his seminal paper on the design of axial flow compressors, "An Aerodynamic Theory of Turbine Design."

After finding a few math errors in Whittle's calculations, Griffith concluded the design was impractical - it was too inefficient, used a pair of as-yet-to-be-developed high-efficiency axial flow compressors, and required high-temperature materials not yet available. Accordingly, he advised the Ministry not to pursue developing the idea further. The Ministry accepted Griffith's conclusions and rejected Whittle's design, notifying him by letter in December 1929.

Griffith and the Air Ministry failed to mention to Whittle that they were developing a similar gas turbine design of their own that required the same high-temperature materials as Whittle's design and that used a Griffith-designed axial flow compressor, which later proved impossibly complex. Moreover, their design, developed at the Air Ministry's lab, used a turbine-driven propeller instead of a jet – a turboprop engine – to power an aircraft. The history of World War II might have been very different had Whittle and Griffith managed to join forces at this time.

Undeterred by the Air Ministry's rejection, Whittle applied for a patent for his turbojet design on 16 January 1930 and was awarded a patent in 1932. But because the Air Ministry professed no official interest in the patent, it was not put on the Secret list and was published worldwide that same year. Forty-six years later, the father of the German jet engine development program, Hans von Ohain, often credited with simultaneously but independently inventing the jet engine in parallel with Whittle, would hint that he'd used some of the information in Whittle's patent to jump-start the German turbojet program starting in 1933, then secretly funded by the government beginning in 1936, and acknowledged Whittle as the true, sole inventor of the turbojet engine.

Between 1934 and 1936, Whittle studied for his Tripos in engineering at Cambridge University under an RAF-sponsored scholarship, famously letting his first patent lapse in 1935 because the Air Ministry, who shared the patent and had unrestricted-user rights, would not help pay the £5 renewal fee.

Whittle, however, doggedly continued to pursue his goal. On 18 May 1935, he applied for a second patent, for an experimental turbojet, which would later be called the W.U, replacing the dual axial flow plus centrifugal compressor combination in his first patent with a single double-sided centrifugal compressor.

On completing his studies, in March 1936, Whittle, along with two ex-RAF officers he'd met at Cambridge, Dudley Williams, and J.C.B. Tinling, and an investment firm, Falk & Partners, launched a company, Power Jets, Ltd., with Whittle acting as chief engineer.

Whittle, still in the RAF – he'd been promoted to flight lieutenant – needed the RAF's permission to work on the turbojet's development. The government, now possibly aware of Germany's jet development program, granted permission and agreed to provide limited support for Whittle's work, receiving 25% of Whittle's share in the company in return.

The W.U design, an experimental engine not intended for flight but only to demonstrate the feasibility of the turbojet concept, was a deceptively simple compressor-turbine combination running on a common shaft, with a single, tubular combustion chamber in between and having only one moving part. And though considered a radical design at the time, it was essentially a turbocharger – something Sanford Moss, a scientist working at General Electric (GE) in Lynn, Massachusetts, had been perfecting since 1919 – but with a kerosene-fueled combustion chamber added between the compressor and turbine sections.

Whittle knew the compressor design was one of the keys to the engine's success. The choice was between: a well-understood but large diameter, high frontal area-high drag centrifugal compressor like that used in GE's turbocharger that required awkward external ducting to route the flow between the sections, reducing efficiency; and a smaller diameter, low frontal area-low drag axial flow compressor with little external ducting but requiring significant engineering development: no one had yet successfully built an axial flow compressor with the required seventy-five percent or greater efficiency to compete with a centrifugal compressor.

Despite the apparent advantages of the axial flow design, to reduce the development effort and risk, Whittle chose the simpler, more-certain centrifugal radial flow design for the demonstration units.

Working on a shoestring budget, Whittle could not afford component-level tests but had to gamble on complete-engine testing. As a result, the first test was of the entire W.U engine, which ran on 12 April 1937.

The design quickly evolved - through three revisions, named First, Second, and Third Models - from a single tubular straight-thru combustion chamber design to a circular array of ten smaller, reverse-flow combustion chambers, with improvements in efficiency and thrust with each model.

After a period of seeming indifference by the government, in June 1939, a demonstration of the W.U Third Model engine, developing a thrust of 1389 pounds-force at 17750 rpm, was made to a delegation from the Air Ministry, most notably, Dr. David R. Pye, the Director of Scientific Research.

The demonstration was so successful the Ministry quickly arranged to buy the engine to give Power Jets some much-needed working capital, then lent it back to them for further testing. They also placed a contract for a flight engine, designated the W.1, a redesigned W.U Third Model with a symmetrical design to facilitate installation in an aircraft.

The Air Ministry also contracted with an airframe manufacturer, Gloster Aircraft Company, to build an experimental aircraft, later designated the Gloster E.28/39, which first flew, using a W.1 engine rated for 849 pounds-force at 16500 rpm, on 15 May 1941.

#

GENERAL ELECTRIC AND THE DEVELOPMENT OF THE J47 TURBOJET ENGINE

In April 1941, the commanding general of the USAAF, General Henry H. "Hap" Arnold, on a goodwill trip to the UK, met Whittle at a secret meeting held by Lord Beaverbrook, William M. Aitken, the head of the Ministry of Aircraft Production, at Aitken's estate outside of London.

After Whittle gave a brief presentation of his turbojet design, Aitken, one of Churchill's most intimate advisors, pulled Arnold aside and bluntly asked,

"What would you do if Churchill was hanged and the rest of us were hiding in Scotland or being run over by the Germans? What would the people in America do? We are against the mightiest army the world has ever seen."

Those present were all in agreement that Germany could invade England anytime it was willing to make the sacrifice.

At the time, the US was a neutral country, not at war with the Axis powers. But whatever assurances Arnold unofficially gave, Great Britain agreed to turn over all the plans for Whittle's turbojet engine to the US, provided utmost secrecy was maintained and a strictly limited number of people were involved in its development.

Arnold inspected Whittle's engine several weeks before its first flight, then witnessed a test flight in mid-May 1941 before arranging to have General Electric's Supercharger Division in West Lynn, Massachusetts, take on the American development of Whittle's prototype.

Tradition says Arnold selected General Electric because the company had relevant turbocharger and high-temperature metallurgy experience and because the administration wanted no interference with the aircraft engine production needed to meet Roosevelt's May 1940 call for 50,000 planes a year.

But some say Arnold had another concern, that if he gave the job to a traditional aircraft piston-engine manufacturer, it might suffer fatally from the same “not-invented-here” syndrome experienced by Whittle. At the time, GE was not an aircraft engine manufacturer, though it was now destined to become the largest in the world.

In early October 1941, the USAAF, using a B-24 bomber and with the highest level of secrecy, delivered the working but unairworthy W.1x engine, a set of the W.2b-revision drawings, and a Power Jets team of three to General Electric in Lynn, Massachusetts, beginning turbojet engine development in the United States.

Arnold’s decision to select General Electric was an informed one. The USAAF had been supporting GE’s turbocharger development since 1917, led by their chief scientist, Sanford Moss, an expert in gas turbines. The turbocharger used an engine’s hot waste exhaust gas to drive a turbine wheel on a common shaft with a centrifugal compressor, boosting the engine’s inlet air pressure without consuming any engine power.

The turbocharger ran very hot, though. Moss's critical breakthrough was to divert cooling air from the compressor to the turbine wheel to keep the metal temperatures within the safe operating limits of the proprietary, high-temperature metals used, like Hastelloy B for the turbine blades and Timken alloy for the turbine disks.

Moss's cooling-air idea and the use of GE's proprietary alloys, unavailable in the UK, would be applied to Whittle's W.2b design to quadruple its rated thrust and increase its overhaul life from 25 hours to several thousand hours.

With the arrival of the Whittle W.1x engine, a set of W.2b drawings, and the Power Jets team, a small dedicated GE team began the intensive, secret development of the first US jet engine, initially designated by GE as the Type I.

The aerodynamic design and most of the mechanical features were identical to the W.2b. However, there were some differences, mainly with the design of the wheel case, which was brought in line with the US practice of mounting engine accessories to the engine itself.

In November 1941, well before the Type I was available for testing, GE began ground running the W.1x engine. This was the first time a jet engine ran in the US, and it allowed GE to gain valuable experience testing a turbojet engine under the supervision of the Power Jets engineers.

On 18 April 1942, twenty-eight weeks after the start of development, GE engineers successfully ran the first Type I engine, though the engine stalled before full power was reached.

With their vast experience developing turbochargers, the GE engineers turned their expertise to improving the Type I design and, at Whittle's suggestion, incorporated partitions in the blower casing to direct airflow into the individual combustion chambers.

The new design, designated the Type I-A, successfully ran on 18 May 1942, developing 1250 pounds-force of thrust and an overall pressure ratio of 3:1.

Further refinements in the Type I-A engine resulted in the Type I-14 design, producing 1400 pounds-force of thrust, and finally, the Type I-16, which the USAAF now designated the J31, developing 1600 pounds-force of thrust. The first US production jet fighter, the Bell P-59 Aracomet, was powered by twin J31 engines and first flew on 1 October 1942, reaching a top speed of 413 mph.

These design improvements were shared with Rolls-Royce, who assumed responsibility for the W.2b engine development and production in the UK on 1 April 1943. Rolls-Royce changed the designation of the W.2b to the Welland I, and twin Welland Is were used to power the UK's first production jet fighter, the Gloster Meteor I, which first flew on 12 January 1944, with a top speed of 417 mph.

GE continued to improve on the basic Type I-A centrifugal compressor design, ultimately resulting in the J33, producing 4000 pounds-force of thrust. It was used in the first US jet fighter to see combat: the single-engine Lockheed P-80 Shooting Star, with a top speed of 594 mph.

In 1943, while developing the axial T31 turboprop engine design, GE recognized they had acquired, working with NACA, the expertise to design an axial flow version of the J33 centrifugal compressor turbojet they were then developing.

They had assisted NACA with their recent research of axial flow compressors culminating in the secret, seminal Report 758 titled, “Performance of Eight-Stage NACA Axial Flow Compressor Designed on the Basis of Airfoil Theory,” providing the high-speed thrust bearings needed for the experiment.

The report showed that multi-stage axial flow compressors could be designed with efficiencies exceeding those of centrifugal compressors, using the NACA-developed equations based on airfoil theory.

GE applied the NACA equations, determined from results for the 14-inch diameter, 8-stage NACA design, with a pressure ratio of 3.4:1, to the design of the axial flow compressor for the 37-

inch diameter T31 design, with a required pressure ratio of 5.3:1, resulting in an increase in the number of stages to 14.

With the measured T31 compressor performance as predicted, GE then used the equations to design the axial flow compressor for the 37-inch diameter J35, an axial flow compressor version of the J33 engine, but only requiring a pressure ratio of 5:1, reducing the number of stages from the T31's 14 to 11.

The improvements gained in going from the 50.5-inch diameter J33's centrifugal design to the J35's axial flow design were: a 46% reduction in frontal area; a 31% reduction in rpm; a 14% increase in pressure ratio; and a 21% increase in thrust, to 5600 pounds-force at 8000 rpm.

Though these improvements were significant, and eventually 14,000 units were produced, GE considered the J35 an experimental design and started developing a more robust, fuel-efficient, longer overhaul life, 5970 pounds-thrust version, the legendary J47 turbojet engine.

The engine first ran on 21 June 1947. It was the first axial flow jet engine approved for commercial use in the US, with over 36,500 units produced, and was in operational service for over 30 years. *Flight Magazine* once described it as the most widely used American-conceived turbojet. First flown in May 1948, just two years later, it would play a pivotal role in the Korean war.

CHAPTER 2 - DEVELOPMENT OF THE NORTH AMERICAN AVIATION F-86A JET FIGHTER

XFJ-1 FURY AND CROSSROADS DECISION

In 1944, the US Navy, in preparation for an invasion of Japan in late 1945, invited US aircraft manufacturers to submit proposals for a jet-powered, carrier-based fighter.

Later that year, on 11 September 1944, the USAAF released the General Operation Requirements for a new day-fighter having a top speed of 600 mph, a combat radius of 705 miles, armament of six .50 caliber machine guns, and using a single General Electric J35 engine.

To satisfy both the Navy and USAAF requirements, North American Aviation (NAA), famed for producing the P-51 Mustang fighter and the B-25 Mitchell bomber, submitted a design they internally designated the NA-134.

The design was based on the wings and tail of the P-51. And, like its competitors, the Lockheed P-80 Shooting Star and the Republic P-84 Thunderjet, used a single turbojet engine: the J33 in the case of the P-80; and the J35 in both the P-84 and the NA-134. The three designs were also aerodynamically similar in that they all used a straight wing.

In January 1945, the Navy placed an order with North American for three prototypes, designated the XFJ-1 Fury, followed by a USAAF order in May for three prototypes of a day-fighter version, designated the XP-86.

The XFJ-Fury first flew on 11 September 1946, reaching a speed of 478 mph, Mach .63, at sea level, and 550 mph, Mach .75, at 10,000 feet, with a maximum service ceiling of 32,000 feet.

These were disappointing results compared to the performance of the other two fighters, which could reach the USAAF's 600 mph requirement. And unlike North American Aviation's lagging development, Lockheed and Republic were in full-production, with the USAAF having already placed contracts with both for production models.

North American was now at a crossroads. They could either scrap the project or risk the further delay of a major redesign. But, with a redesign, they could benefit from a late start by incorporating recently captured German aerodynamic research data on thin, swept wings and details of the ME262 design that could lead to a radical, much more aerodynamically advanced fighter design, leapfrogging their competition.

The firm had faced a similar decision in early 1940 when it had been invited to manufacture Curtis P-40s under license for the

British. Instead, company president James H. Kindelberger and chief engineer John L. Atwood opted to design a better fighter, resulting in the iconic P-51 Mustang. They decided to take a similar risk again.

#

XP-86 AND SWEPT-WING DESIGN

North American's engineers pored over the captured design documents of the ME262, looking for reasons for the fighter's low drag when operating at high Mach number, near the speed of sound, in the transonic flow region. The answer appeared to lie with the plane's 18.5-degree swept-wing design.

Adolf Busemann worked as an aeronautical research scientist at Germany's Max-Plank Institute in the early 1930s. He was a member of the famed team there - led by Ludwig Prandtl, Theodore von Karman, Max Munk, and Jacob Ackeret - and is credited with being the first to discover the benefits of a swept-wing design for high-speed aircraft. He presented his seminal paper on the topic at the Volta Conference in Rome in 1935.

The paper, however, was only concerned with supersonic flow, and with the landplane airspeed record of 352 mph having just been set two weeks earlier by Howard Hughes, it was considered an academic curiosity and soon forgotten by all the attendees. Nevertheless, Busemann continued working with the concept and, by the end of 1935, had demonstrated similar benefits in the transonic region as well.

During the war, Busemann became director of the secret German Aeronautical Research Institute (LFA) in Braunschweig, Germany, and started a series of experimental wind tunnel tests there of the swept-wing concept. By 1942, he had amassed a considerable amount of useful technical data at a time when Germany was desperately gambling on advanced high-speed aircraft to turn the tide of the war.

Soon after WWII ended in Europe, a team of American aerodynamicists, including George S. Schairer from Boeing, traveled to Germany and reached the Braunschweig labs on 7 May 1945. There they found Busemann and a mass of data on the swept-wing concept. When they questioned Busemann about it, his face lit up, and he said,

"Oh, you remember, I read a paper on it at the Volta Conference in 1935."

Several team members, including Schairer, remembered the presentation but had forgotten all the details of the paper. Now realizing its importance, Schairer immediately wrote Boeing and told them to investigate the concept. As a result, the B-47 Stratojet bomber's wing and tail were redesigned to include a 35-degree backward sweep.

The captured swept-wing data was shared with the other US military aircraft manufacturers, including North American Aviation, who was now using it to reverse engineer the ME262, to figure out why the German designers had settled on an 18.5-degree sweep angle.

Incredibly, what they discovered was that the swept-wing design was not initially included for aerodynamic reasons. Instead, it was an inelegant solution to a center-of-gravity problem created by the pair of heavier-than-expected BMW 003 jet engines, late replacements for the Jumo 004 engines that proved unreliable. Sweeping the wings back 18.5 degrees moved the center-of-gravity aft the right amount to compensate for the heavier engines.

Only after the swept-wing change had been made did wind tunnel tests show the advantage of the swept-wing design in lowering the drag at high Mach number. Unfortunately, Busemann's data was unavailable to the ME262's designers, so they did not attempt to optimize the sweep angle.

According to Busemann, a swept wing works by increasing the critical Mach number, or speed at which the air flowing over the wing, becomes sonic, forming a shock wave on the wing's top surface near the leading edge, significantly increasing the drag of the wing and destroying its lift.

A swept-wing design delays the onset of a shock wave by changing the apparent speed of the airstream impacting the leading edge of the wing, turning the air velocity into two components: one in the direction normal to the wing; and one in the direction lateral to the wing. Only the normal-direction velocity component, which is slower than the aircraft's airspeed, contributes to the development of a shock wave, so a plane with a given airfoil-shaped wing can fly faster with a swept wing than with a straight wing.

The disadvantage of a swept-wing design is that, for the same reasons, the wing will stall – produce no lift - at a higher airspeed. The ME262's designers realized this and, to compensate, added leading edge slats, or flaps, to the wings that automatically deployed at slow airspeed to increase the wings' lift.

Since the XP-86 was intended to fly at Mach .95 or greater, in the transonic flow region, North American's engineers chose, from Busemann's research data, the optimum sweep angle for that airspeed, 35 degrees, to sweep both the wings and the tail section.

And they used a much thinner airfoil shape for the wings - 30% less than the Fury's and 14% less than the ME262's. They also incorporated the ME262's automatically deploying leading edge slats in the design of the swept wings.

The other feature North American's engineers borrowed from the ME262 design was an electrically-adjustable, fully-moveable horizontal stabilizer whose incline to the airstream could be adjusted for trimming the pitch. In later models, the stabilizer design would evolve into a full-flying tail, or stabilator, which provided much greater control in the transonic and supersonic flight regions.

North American's chief designer, Edgar Schmued, who had been given the opportunity to examine a captured ME262, led the XP-86 design effort and, along with a team of over 500 engineers, incorporated the latest advances in jet fighter engine and airframe technology – like an ejector seat, and hydraulically-actuated speed breaks - into the XP-86 design, resulting in the most advanced jet fighter the world had ever seen, the legendary F-86 Sabre jet.

The first prototype was completed at North American's Inglewood, CA, plant on 8 August 1947, just two years from the start of the contract, and was trucked to a remote desert test facility, Muroc AFB, CA, for flight tests.

The GE J35 engine powered the initial prototypes, but production models were powered by the more advanced and recently available GE J47 axial flow turbojet engine.

The XP-86 first flew on 1 October 1947, with a rated top speed of 685 mph, a maximum service ceiling of 49,600 feet, and a range of 1200 miles with drop tanks.

#

F-86A TURBOJET PRODUCTION AND INITIAL DEPLOYMENT

Government officials were very impressed with the fighter's performance and quickly moved to place an order with North American. By the end of the year, a contract was signed, and work began on 33 production models, designated the F-86A Sabre.

The fighter was so fast that, on 26 April 1948, in a shallow dive, it may have broken the sound barrier, two weeks before Chuck Yeager officially did. Though only rated as a transonic aircraft, later versions with more powerful J47 engines routinely flew supersonic, requiring modifications to the tail to improve flight control.

On 15 September 1948, USAF Major Richard L. Johnson, flying an F-86A, officially broke the world speed record, flying straight and level at 671 mph. Later versions would break the record again, at 699 mph and then at 716 mph.

The F-86s began to be deployed in February 1949, first going to the 1st Fighter Group's 94th Fighter Squadron stationed at March Field AFB, CA. After that, the USAF initiated full-scale production, and by January 1950, three state-side USAF fighter groups – the 1st, 4th, and 8th – had all been equipped with F-86As. In total, the USAF had procured 554 production models, with the last delivered in December 1950. By then, however, the Sabre was fully engaged in combat.

#

INTO THE BREACH

On 25 June 1950, the forces of North Korea attacked south of the 38th Parallel, and the US joined other United Nations (UN) members in a "police action" that quickly escalated into a full-blown war.

The US Air Force (USAF) Far East Air Forces supplied F-80s, F-84s, and F-51s, mainly used as fighter-bombers, whose designations had been changed from -P- for pursuit interceptor to -F- for fighter when the USAF became a separate branch of the services in 1947.

In November 1950, F-51 Mustangs attacking an enemy airfield just south of the Yalu River were jumped by Chinese pilots flying new jet-powered, Russian-built, MiG-15s.

The piston engine-propeller-driven WWII-era F-51 fighters were no match for the MiGs, and neither were the jet-powered F-

80 Shooting Stars and F-84 Thunderjets, which were 100 mph slower than the MiGs.

In response, the USAF rushed the F-86A Sabres of the 4th Fighter Group to Kimpo AB near Seoul, South Korea.

Elements of the Group arrived on 17 December 1950, and, with the North Korean army approaching and only 12 miles from Seoul, immediately engaged with the enemy and fought off the attacking MiGs, downing one MiG in the process and incurring no losses. Other Sabre units followed, and before long, the USAF was claiming a kill ratio of 14:1, attributing most of the credit for the victories to the F-86.

USAF pilots flying the F-86 in Korea eventually claimed a total of 792 MiG aerial kills versus a loss of 78 F-86s. Some historians argue that the victories were overstated and that the kill ratio was really closer to 1:1. Others say that even if the kill ratio was high, it was the superior training of the US pilots versus the North Korean or even Chinese pilots that made the difference. The truth may never be known.

The air battle over Korea was a fiercely fought one, maybe even tougher on the pilots than the one over Europe during WWII. The two premier jet fighters were evenly matched, with the speed advantage going to the F-86 and the rate-of-climb and service ceiling advantage going to the MiG-15.

The MiG-15s were better armed, carrying two 23 mm and one 37 mm cannon firing heavy, destructive explosive shells designed to destroy the B-29 bombers, but fired at a slow rate, versus the F-86, which carried six M3 .50-caliber machine guns firing lead bullets but at a much faster rate. In addition, the MiG's armament was more destructive – a single hit could down an F-86, while it took multiple strikes from an F-86 to down a MiG – but the F-86's radar-guided gunsight was much more advanced, so aiming of the F-86's guns was far superior.

For most of the war, the dogfighting occurred near the 38th Parallel, in an area called MiG Alley, which was 200 miles north of the F-86 bases, but just a few miles south of the MiG bases, so the MiG's had the advantage of fighting on their home turf, where they could quickly rearm and refuel. And the Russians provided substantially more MiGs than the US did F-86s, so the MiGs also had the numerical advantage.

The US pilots were well-trained, and many were experienced veterans of WWII. But so were the Russian pilots who secretly flew for the North Koreans for most of the war.

What is not in dispute is that the F-86 was inserted into the breach in Korea, arriving just in time to prevent the routing of the United Nations forces there, ultimately resulting in a stalemate instead of total defeat for the UN. Maybe it's for this reason that the Sabre emerged as the undisputed champion of the war.

The Sabre's record in Korea established it as the premier fighter of its generation and that its pilots were a match for any pilots flying first-line Soviet aircraft. The Cold War would continue, but the Soviet Union's experience in Korea taught it to think twice before testing the US Air Force again.

A total of 9860 F-86s were produced, with only an estimated 24 airworthy planes remaining. But hundreds of Sabers are on static display in museums worldwide that could be scavenged for parts, hopefully enough to keep examples of the F-86 Sabre jet flying well into the next century.

CHAPTER 3 – BRIEF HISTORY OF THE 4TH FIGHTER-INTERCEPTOR WING AND ITS SERVICE IN THE KOREAN AIR WAR

BIRTH OF THE 4TH FIGHTER GROUP AND ITS SERVICE IN WWII: 19 SEPTEMBER 1940 – 10 NOVEMBER 1945

The 4th Fighter Wing's history as one of the most distinguished fighter units in the world spans more than 50 years and five wars, going back to the beginning of WWII.

In September 1939, an American mercenary pilot, Colonel Charles Sweeney, began raising a squadron of volunteer civilians to fly for the RAF in Europc.

Under American law, it was illegal for US citizens to join the armed services of another country: joining the RAF could cost the US volunteers their citizenship. Regardless, financed by Sweeney, over thirty American volunteers made their way to France to join the RAF before Germany invaded France in early May 1940.

None of the initial group of volunteers got to fly while in France, but several made their way to England when the British evacuated France in late May 1940 and flew in the RAF during the Battle of Britain from 10 July to 31 October 1940.

Sweeney's nephew, also named Charles, approached Britain's Air Ministry in July 1940 about forming separate American squadrons for those serving with the RAF. The Air Ministry adopted the idea and agreed that the handful of Americans already serving with the RAF and any new recruits would be formed into their own national units, to be known as Eagle Squadrons.

The first of these Eagle units, the 71st Squadron, was formed on 19 September 1940, followed by the 121st and the 133rd. The squadrons, flying Hurricanes and Spitfires, were quickly filled with 250 new American volunteers recruited and smuggled to England over the next 12 months by the Sweeneys and another American group with the same mission, the Clayton Knight Committee. Both groups worked together but in secret, against American law, though some suspect with the tacit approval of President Franklin Roosevelt.

After the US entered WWII, with the arrival of the USAAF Eighth Air Force in England, the RAF Eagle Squadron units and the men serving in them were transferred to the Eighth Air Force forming, on 12 September 1942, the 4th Fighter Group, with three squadrons, designated the 334th, the 335th, and the 336th.

The 4th Fighter Group was stationed at Debden Airfield, officially known as Station 356, in the small rural village of Debden in the Uttlesford district of Essex, UK, about 17 miles south-southeast of Cambridge. The Group initially flew Spitfires but changed to P-47 Thunderbolts in March 1943, providing escort protection for the Eighth's bombers to and from the German frontier. Later, in April 1944, the Group switched to long-range P-51 Mustangs extending their bomber protection to include Germany as well.

From its formation, the Group was a record-setter. Earning its motto, "Fourth but First," it was the first to use belly tanks, the first to penetrate Germany, the first to escort bombers to Berlin, and the first to shoot down an ME262 jet fighter.

The group escorted USAF bombers that attacked factories, submarine pens, V-weapon sights, and other targets in France, the Low Countries, and Germany. And it flew raids against the Luftwaffe, strafing and dive-bombing German airfields while also hitting troops, supply depots, roads, bridges, rail lines, and trains.

The Group participated in Operation Argument, Big Week, from 20 to 25 February 1944, escorting Eighth Air Force bombers attacking German aircraft, engine, and ball-bearing plants. In addition, they flew interdictory and counter-air missions during the

D-Day invasion of Normandy in June 1944; supported the airborne invasion of Holland in September 1944; participated in the Battle of the Bulge from 16 December 1944 to 25 January 1945; and covered the airborne assault across the Rhine in March 1945.

For its aggressiveness in seeking out and destroying German aircraft and air bases from 5 March to 24 April 1944, the 4th Fighter Group received a Distinguished Unit Citation (DUC).

The Group flew its last mission of the war on 25 April 1945 and was credited with a total of 583 air-to-air victories, more than any other Eighth Air Force unit, producing 38 Aces. Pilot losses were 125 killed-in-action and 105 prisoners-of-war of 553 pilots serving, for a 42% attrition rate.

Two of the Group's top Aces were USAAF Captains Don Gentile and John Godfrey.

Gentile joined the RAF 133 Eagle Squadron after going to Canada for training in 1940; he was with the squadron when it converted to the 334th Fighter Squadron in September 1942. Godfrey was Gentile's close friend and wingman. General Dwight

D. Eisenhower referred to Gentile as a one-man Air Force, while Winston Churchill referred to the pair as the Damon and Pythias of the twentieth century.

Soon after the war, in the rush to demobilize, the 4th Fighter Group was deactivated at Camp Kilmer, NJ, on 10 November 1945. Unfortunately, they wouldn't remain deactivated for long.

#

INTERWAR YEARS: 15 AUGUST 1945 – 25 JUNE 1950

After the end of WWII, on 15 August 1945, the US accepted the surrender of the Japanese forces in Korea south of the 38th Parallel, while the Soviet Union accepted the Japanese surrender north of that line. Although the Western Allies – the US, Great Britain, and France - intended that Korea become an independent democracy, the Soviet Union had other plans.

Close allies during the war, tensions between the Soviet Union and the Western Allies quickly began to grow as the Soviet

Union, aware of the US's rapid demobilization and lack of resolve to stay to defend Europe against Soviet aggression, began pressing to extend its sphere of influence.

Winston Churchill, in a speech at Westminster College in Fulton, Missouri, on 5 March 1946, warned,

"*From Stettin in the Baltic to Trieste in the Adriatic, an Iron Curtain has descended across the Continent. Behind that line lie all the capitals of the ancient states of Central and Eastern Europe. Warsaw, Berlin, Prague, Vienna, Budapest, Belgrade, Bucharest, and Sofia; all these famous cities and the populations around them lie in what I must call the Soviet sphere, and all are subject, in one form or another, not only to Soviet influence but to a very high and in some cases increasing measure of control from Moscow.*" The Cold War had begun.

In a speech to a joint session of Congress on 12 March 1947, President Harry S. Truman announced what became known as the Truman Doctrine, offering financial aid and implying American military support for nations threatened by Soviet communism. The Truman Doctrine became the foundation of American policy and directly led to the formation of the North Atlantic Treaty Organization (NATO) in 1949.

The Selective Service Act expired that same month, and Truman pushed Congress to extend the draft. The Act was reenacted in June 1948. More than 1.5 million men would later be inducted into the armed services during the Korean War through this Act.

The National Security Act of 1947 reorganized the military into the Department of the Army, the Department of the Navy, the Marine Corps, and the newly created Department of the Air Force, making the Air Force an independent branch of service from the Army. And on 14 April 1948, Truman signed an executive order establishing the Air Force Reserves.

Within the next 18 months: the Soviet Union blockaded Berlin and detonated its first atomic bomb; communist Chinese forces defeated the Nationalist forces and forced their retreat to the island of Formosa, establishing the People's Republic of China; the

Soviet Union created the German Democratic Republic government in East Germany; and Russia signed the Treaty of Friendship, Alliance, and Mutual Assistance with the new communist Chinese government.

Back in 1947, the US had put the problems of Korean unification and independence before the United Nations. When the UN ordered free elections throughout the country, the Soviet Union refused to allow them in the north. Free elections in the southern half of Korea in May 1948 established the Republic of Korea, and the UN recognized it as the legitimate government for all of Korea. The Soviets then created a rival communist government in the north, the People's Democratic Republic of Korea.

With governments established in both halves of Korea, the Soviets announced their intention to leave the country and challenged the US to do the same.

After training a small national force for internal security in South Korea, the US departed, leaving only a few military advisers.

In the North, the Soviets oversaw the creation of a well-trained North Korean People's Army equipped with Soviet tanks, heavy artillery, and aircraft. After assuring the military superiority of North Korea, the Soviets left in 1949. Less than a year later, border skirmishes between the North and South exploded into an all-out war.

#

SUMMARY OF THE F-86 SABRE IN THE KOREAN AIR WAR: 25 JUNE 1950 – 27 JULY 1953

In the early morning hours of Sunday, 25 June 1950, the forces of North Korea invaded the South. Unfortunately, the South Korean army was poorly organized and badly led, and the initial North Korean advance was quite rapid.

That same day, the United Nations Security Council met in Emergency Session and ordered the North Koreans to cease their invasion and withdraw from the South, but these demands were ignored. The Soviet Union, though, boycotting the UN because it failed to recognize communist China, was not present to veto the action.

On 27 June, President Truman, adhering to the Truman Doctrine, authorized American forces to oppose the invasion. US Army General Douglas MacArthur ordered the USAF Far East Air Force (FEAF) into immediate action against the North Koreans. Truman also began the mobilization of the Reserves.

According to USAF Lieutenant General E. George Stratemeyer, Far East Air Forces Commander during the first year of the war,

"As it happened, the air battle was short and sweet. Air supremacy over Korea was quickly established."

The UN pilots who flew in Korea and experienced some of the fiercest air battles ever fought may have had a very different view.

At the start of the war, the combat units of the FEAF were equipped with the Lockheed F-80 Shooting Star jet fighter, the North American F-82 Twin Mustang all-weather escort fighter, the Douglas B-26 Invader light attack bomber, the Lockheed RF-80A tactical reconnaissance aircraft, and the Boeing B-29 Superfortress heavy bomber. These were soon supplemented by North American F-51 Mustang fighters quickly transferred from the US.

These US aircraft rapidly gained control of the air from the Korean People's Armed Forces Air Corp (KPAFAC), which was equipped with an assortment of Russian-built WWII-era aircraft, including the Yakolev Yak-9 and Lavochkin La-11 fighters, the Ilyushin I1-10 ground attack aircraft, and a smattering of Yak-18 and Po-2 trainers.

Having quickly and almost completely eliminated the KPAFAC, the FEAF turned to ground attack to try and halt the rapid North Korean army advance.

Despite repeated air attacks by UN aircraft on the advancing North Korean troops, though, by early September, the UN armies had been squeezed down into a small pocket south of the Naktong River, in the southeast corner of the country known as the Pusan Perimeter. As a result, there was genuine concern that the hard-pressed UN troops might be forced to evacuate the entire Korean peninsula.

General MacArthur's flanking and amphibious invasion maneuver at Inchon on 15 September 1950 suddenly reversed the fortunes of the UN forces in Korea. By the end of the month, the North Korean forces had been driven entirely out of South Korea.

The UN then decided to enforce its prewar intention of reuniting all of Korea under one government. Accordingly, UN forces advanced across the 38th Parallel and headed north into

North Korea, despite stern warnings from China of possible intervention if UN troops approached their border.

By the end of October, UN forces were near the Chinese-Manchurian frontier, and some forward units were on the southern banks of the Yalu River at the Manchurian border.

On 1 November 1950, a group of F-51s and B-26s were bombing and strafing an airfield near Sinuiju, just across the Yalu River from China, when they encountered six swept-wing jets coming across the river at them, firing as they approached.

The Mustangs were able to escape the attack and return to base to report the arrival of the MiG-15 in Korea.

The Russian-built MiG-15 was originally designed as a high-altitude interceptor to counter the US B-29 and B-36 long-range bombers. The prototype made its first flight on 30 December 1947, powered by an imported Rolls-Royce Nene centrifugal flow turbojet engine, which was naively sold to the Russians by the British as a goodwill gesture, quickly reverse-engineered by the Soviets, and produced by them as the RD-45.

The first production of MiG-15s reached operational units in early 1949. However, the RD-45 proved unreliable and had a high fuel consumption. Later variants of the MiG-15s, known as the MiGbis, used the Klimov VK-1 engine, an improved version of the RD-45, providing 5957 pounds-force of thrust. These entered operational service in early 1950 and eventually became the most widely produced version of the MiG.

Armament consisted of one 37 mm cannon with 40 rounds and two 23 mm cannons with 80 rounds each.

The early MiGs in Korea were not flown by Chinese or North Korean pilots but by experienced Russians, many veterans of WWII.

In February 1950, the Russian 29th Fighter Aviation Regiment was transferred from Moscow to China. The 15th Fighter Aviation Division later joined it to form the 64th Fighter Aviation Corps. The 64th was committed to combat in Korea in November 1950.

The Corps' pilots wore Chinese uniforms to conceal direct Russian involvement in the war and were not allowed to speak Russian over the radio. This deception continued until the summer of 1951 when Chinese and North Korean pilots began to fly the MiGs in combat.

In these early encounters, the Russian MiG pilots would cross the border at high altitude, dive down and attack UN aircraft, then duck back over the Yalu River. They knew that, for political reasons, the UN aircraft were forbidden to follow.

On 8 November 1950, the first jet-versus-jet battle took place when USAF Lieutenant Russel J. Brown, flying an F-80C, shot down one out of a flight of four MiG-15s that had dashed across the Yalu.

Even though the F-80C had managed to draw first blood, the MiG was reported to be 100 miles faster than the F-80C Shooting Star. As a result, the USAF realized that the MiG-15s posed a significant threat: they could wrest control of the air from the UN forces if left unchecked.

This threat was soon confirmed when the Chinese-based MiGs began attacking the B-29 bombers flying near the Chinese border. The F-80 escort fighters proved too slow to provide effective protection, causing temporary suspension of the B-29 daylight bombing campaign.

To counter the MiG threat, on 8 November 1950, the 4th Fighter-Interceptor Wing - equipped with the F-86A Sabre jets and consisting of the 334th, the 335th, and the 336th Fighter-Interceptor Squadrons (FISs), based at Dover AFB, Wilmington, DE, - was ordered to Korea. Most of the 4th's pilots were seasoned WWII veterans who combined had shot down over 1000 German aircraft during the war.

The 334th and 335th FISs flew to San Diego, and their planes were loaded aboard a Navy escort carrier. The 336th FIS went to San Francisco and was loaded aboard a tanker.

The 336th's F-86As arrived in Japan first on 26 November 1950 and were unloaded that same day. Seven of the aircraft were immediately serviced and, as soon as they were ready, flown to

Kimpo Air Base (AB), USAF designation K-14, in Korea near Seoul, arriving on 13 December 1950.

Before any Sabres had reached Korea, however, on 26 November 1950, the Chinese army intervened with devastating force, breaking through the UN lines and throwing the UN army back into utter chaos.

The MiGs did not provide any air support for this invasion, having been unable to establish an effective intervention zone below a narrow strip near the Yalu, what became known as MiG Alley. Had the MiGs established and held air superiority over the battle area, the UN forces may have been forced to evacuate Korea.

The first Sabre mission took place on 17 December 1950. It was an armed reconnaissance of the region just south of the Yalu. The commander of the 4th Wing's 336th Squadron succeeded in shooting down one MiG out of a flight of four to score first blood for the Sabre.

During December, the 4th Wing flew 234 sorties, engaged with the enemy 76 times, and scored eight victories, with the loss of one aircraft.

By the end of 1950, the combined Chinese and North Korean armies had driven the UN forces out of North Korea and begun invading the South. As a result, the Sabres were forced to leave Kimpo and evacuate to Johnson AB, Japan, which put them out of range of the action up along the Yalu.

Even though the Yalu was now out of range, on 14 January 1951, an F-86A detachment arrived at Taegu AB in the southeast corner of South Korea, operating as fighter-bombers to try and halt the Chinese and North Korean advance.

Eventually, the Chinese-North Korean advance halted due to over-extended supply lines and the relentless UN air attacks. By the end of January, the UN forces began pushing them back north, and on 10 February 1951, Kimpo AB was retaken, followed by Seoul on 3 March. By 1 April, all the Chinese-North Korean forces had been driven out of South Korea and pushed back above the 38th Parallel.

The halting of the Chinese-North Korean army's advance can be primarily attributed to the inability of the MiGs to provide any effective support for the attack. Not only had no Chinese bombers appeared to attack UN troops, but no MiGs had flown south of the Yalu region to attack the UN aircraft that were relentlessly bombing and strafing the Chinese-North Korean armies.

The Chinese and North Koreans had plans for a major spring offensive to drive the UN out of Korea. The plans were based on the construction of a series of North Korean air bases and for the Chinese-based MiGs to use these bases to gain air supremacy over the North, preventing UN aircraft from interfering with the offensive.

In early March, the MiGs became more active in support of this offensive. On March 1, MiGs jumped a formation of nine B-29s and severely damaged three of them. Fortunately, by this time, the UN base at Suwon was ready, and Sabres could return to Korea and reenter the fray over the Yalu.

An advanced detachment of Sabres from the 4th Wing's 334th Squadron began their patrols along the Yalu from Suwon AB on 6 March, followed four days later by the rest of the squadron. At the same time, the 4th's 336th Squadron moved to Taegu AB from Japan so they could stage Sabres through Suwon AB. The 4th Wing's other squadron, the 335th, would remain in Japan until 7 May, when they moved to Suwon AB to join the 4th's other two squadrons.

The Sabres would arrive for their 25-minute patrol in five-minute intervals. They'd usually find the MiGs cruising back and forth along the river at high-altitude on the other side of the Yalu, looking for the best time to attack. However, the MiGs would often remain on the north side of the river, tantalizingly out of reach of the Sabres.

When the MiGs did choose to engage, the Sabres would have only a fleeting moment to fire at the MiGs before they broke off and escaped back across the Yalu.

The MiGs had the advantage of being able to choose the time and place of combat. The MiG-15 had a better high-altitude performance than the F-86A, having a higher combat ceiling and a higher climb rate, and was faster at higher altitudes than the F-86A. Its superior high-altitude performance enabled the MiG to break off combat at will.

The F-86 pilots were far more experienced, though, than their Chinese and North Korean opponents and were better marksmen. And the Sabre was a more stable gun platform with fewer high-speed instabilities than the MiG. In addition, the F-86A was faster than the MiG-15 at lower altitudes, and an effective strategy was for a Sabre pilot to force the battle down to lower altitudes where the Sabre had the advantage.

In April, the MiGs got a lot bolder and attempted to intercept B-29 formations attacking targets in the Sinuiju area near the Yalu. The biggest air battle of that spring occurred on 12 April 1951, when over 70 MiGs attacked a formation of 39 B-29s escorted by F-84s and F-86s. Three B-29s were lost versus 14 MiGs destroyed, four by Sabres and ten by the B-29's gunners.

No F-86As were lost in air-to-air action during the first five months of 1951, though they flew 3550 sorties and scored 22 victories. Most of the attrition was caused by accidents rather than by losses in combat.

In June, the MiGs became even more aggressive, and their pilots seemed more skilled. One Sabre was lost on 11 June when the 4th Wing, covering an F-80 attack on the Sinuiju airfield, shot down two more MiGs. Six MiGs were destroyed in air battles between 17-19 June, with two Sabres lost.

As the first year of the Korean War ended, it was apparent that the Sabre had been instrumental in frustrating the MiG-15's bid for air superiority. Without control of the air, the Chinese and North Koreans could not establish their series of North Korean bases, so they could not carry out any effective air support for their spring offensive. The result was the war settled into a stalemate on the ground.

The more-advanced F-86E began to enter service in Korea with the 4th Wing in July 1951, replacing the F-86As on a one-by-one basis. The 4th's conversion was relatively slow, though, and the last F-86A was not replaced until July 1952.

In September 1951, MiG-15bis began to appear, powered by a 6000 pounds-force engine.

On 22 October 1951, seventy-five F-86Es were shipped to Japan to replace the F-80Cs of the 51st Wing stationed at Suwon AB to meet the new threat of MiG-15bis attacks against the B-29 bombers. The 51st Wing, consisting of the 16th and 25th FIS, began operations with its new F-86Es from Suwon AB on 1 December.

At any one time, only about 60 Sabres could be put into the air, assuming the rest of the Sabre force stationed at Kimpo or Suwon ABs was not on alert or down for maintenance.

Even at maximum level, the Sabre force was far outnumbered by the MiGs. By late 1951, there were enough MiGs available, so the Chinese attempted to move a couple of MiG squadrons into the base at Uiju, North Korea. However, UN air attacks soon made this base untenable, forcing the MiGs back across the Yalu.

The third squadron of Sabres was added to the 51st FIW - the 39th FIS - in June 1952. Even with this increase, in late 1952, MiGs still outnumbered Sabres by about 1000 to 150.

In late 1951, the rules of engagement were modified, allowing UN pilots to cross the Yalu when in hot pursuit of the enemy. However, many Sabre pilots violated the rule, and F-86 pilots flew north of the Yalu looking for MiGs, with more MiG kills scored on the north side of the Yalu than on the south side. The UN Manchurian sanctuary rule was finally rescinded in April 1952.

The first F-86Fs reached Korea in June 1952 and quickly boosted Sabre victories. The 4th Wing's 335th Squadron scored a total of 81 victories during the remainder of 1952, while the other two 4th Wing squadrons, still operating with the F-86E, scored 41. With this success, the USAF goal became to convert all Sabre squadrons to F-86Fs as soon as possible.

Fifty "6-3" wing conversion kits were shipped to Korea in high secrecy in September 1952 to convert F-86F aircraft already there to the new high-Mach number wing configuration.

The "6-3" wing conversion quickly boosted Sabre victories even further. With the "6-3 wing" F-86Fs, the USAF now had a fighter that greatly outclassed the MiGs that: could match the MiG's maximum speed at high-altitude, up to the Sabre's service ceiling of 47,000 feet; could turn inside the MiG; had as good a rate-of-climb; was faster in a dive and at low altitude; and, had much greater endurance.

In late 1952, fully one-fifth of Sabre victories over the MiGs were obtained without the F-86F pilots firing a shot. During the last four months of 1952, thirty-two MiGs were observed to go into sudden uncontrollable spins while being chased by Sabres.

Only two of the MiG pilots managed to recover from the spin. The rest either ejected or crashed with their planes. Many inexperienced MiG pilots were now entering the fray and panicked when chased by the technically-superior Sabres.

With the "6-3" F-86F Sabres, the USAF racked up its highest score against the MiG-15s. Between 8-31 May 1953, F-86Fs scored 56 MiG kills versus one loss, resulting in one of the most lop-sided air battles ever fought.

Facing increasing UN air power pressure, the North Koreans finally signed a ceasefire on 27 July 1953, ending the Korean War.

The merits of the MiG-15 versus the F-86 in Korea have long been debated.

The MiG-15 enjoyed some performance advantages over the early-model F-86A. But it also suffered some serious design flaws that resulted in high-speed instability and the deaths of many of its pilots. And the F-86A was a better gun platform and could dive faster. Ultimately, any MiG performance advantages over the

Sabre were more than offset by the superior training of American pilots.

The actual kill-to-loss ratio of the F-86 to the MiG-15 is still controversial. An official Air Force publication issued just after the war listed 808 MiGs shot down for a loss of 58 Sabres, for a kill ratio of 14:1. Later USAF reports listed 792 MiGs downed versus 78 Sabres lost, for a kill ratio of 10:1. The Soviets claimed a kill ratio of 2:1, in the MiGs favor.

There was a total of 39 Korean War USAF jet Aces. All of them flew the F-86.

The newly-established US Air Force emerged from the Korean War as a proven force, ready to face future Cold War challenges.

In the air war in Korea, 1198 USAF airmen gave their lives.

The Korean War death toll is staggering, with over 5 million killed, half of them civilians. Almost 40,000 Americans died in action, with more than 100,000 wounded.

#

4TH FIGHTER-INTERCEPTOR WING AND ITS SERVICE IN THE KOREAN WAR: 9 SEPTEMBER 1946 – 27 JULY 1953

Less than a year after being deactivated, the 4th Fighter Group was reactivated at Selfridge Field, MI, on 9 September 1946 due to increasing Cold War tensions.

Initially trained on the F-80 Shooting Star jets, the Group transitioned to the F-86A Sabre jet in March 1949, just in time to receive advanced gunnery training before being deployed to fight in the Korean War.

In November 1950, the Group, now designated the 4th Fighter-Interceptor Wing, became the first F-86 fighter wing to be deployed to Korea. During the Wing's first mission, on 17 December 1950, USAF Lieutenant Colonel Bruce H. Hinton shot down a MiG-15. Four days later, USAF Lieutenant Colonel John C. Meyer, a WWII Ace, led flight elements of the Wing into the first all-jet battle in history. The flight elements downed six MiG-15s without sustaining any losses.

Depending on the status of the ground war at the time, the 4th was stationed at multiple air bases: Kimpo AB, South Korea, 15 December 1950; Johnson AB, Japan, 2 January 1951; Suwon AB, South Korea, 7 May 1951; and Kimpo AB, South Korea, 23 August 1951 to 1 October 1954.

In all, the 4th Fighter-Interceptor Wing would claim a total of 502 of the 792 MiGs destroyed in air-to-air combat by the USAF during the Korean War, becoming the top fighter unit of the war. The Wing received two Distinguished Service Citations, and twenty-four of the Wing's pilots achieved Ace status. One Ace pilot, 32-year-old USAF Major George A. Davis, Jr., a WWII veteran and an Ace of that war as well, posthumously received the Congressional Medal of Honor.

Pilot losses were 32 killed-in-action (KIA), with an estimated ten missing-in-action (MIA) or prisoner-of-war (POW).

CHAPTER 4 – BLISS: JULY 1945 - SEPTEMBER 1947

PENOBSCOT BAY: MID-JULY 1945

The 30-foot Alden Malabar Jr.-class yawl easily sliced through the 2-foot-high waves, sailing on a broad reach before the 18-knot southerly breeze, heading northeast towards the 90-foot-tall Matinicus Rock Lighthouse at the entrance to Penobscot Bay, ME. With Jeff at the helm, and Matt working the jib, mizzen, and mainsail sheets, the boat was flying, sailing at nearly its hull speed of 7 knots.

They had left Swampscott, MA, the morning before at 11:00 am for the 120-nautical-mile, 20-hour sail to Maine, planning their estimated arrival time for mid-morning to enter the rocky bay in daylight and to lessen their chance of encountering fog.

Sailing all night on a steady course, with a constant, following wind and with the sails set for the evening, they had little to do other than steer. With a cloudless sky and only a quarter moon, the stars were bright, and the band of the Milky Way was vivid. Trading helm watches every 4 hours, Matt and Jeff had each managed to get some sleep on deck, wrapped in a blanket and with their head resting on the thigh of the one steering.

Both were awake to watch the spectacular sunrise, though. A few minutes before, Jeff had made some coffee in the cabin and brought a mug up on deck to warm Matt, who was nearing the end of his watch. Sharing the mug in silence, they watched the sun's rays peak over the horizon, with an arm draped over each other's shoulder.

For the next two weeks, the two explored the Bay, starting with the small, quaint town of Camden on the west side of the Bay.

The hike to the top of Mount Battie above Camden on the first day was amazing, with a stunning panoramic view of the Bay. They walked the waterfront the next day, stopping for an early breakfast with the hard-working lobstermen, enjoying their thick Down East Maine accent.

The two-day sail east, beginning the following day across the Bay to Mount Desert Island and Arcadia National Park, was equally impressive. They sailed past the large islands of North Haven, Deer Isle, and Swans Island and stopped to explore several of the small, uninhabited islands along the way, having the overnight anchorage of one all to themselves.

The mornings and evenings were chilly and often foggy but made for good sleeping weather, especially cozy for the two, who shared the same flannel-lined L.L. Bean sleeping bag.

The rugged beauty of mid-Coast Maine struck a nerve with them both, and they couldn't do enough hiking and exploring of the area. This was especially true for Jeff, who had never heard of Acadia National Park before, so he didn't know what to expect.

The trail to the top of Cadillac Mountain was especially stunning. It wove through the lush, mixed deciduous and boreal forest teaming with wildlife and offered magnificent scenic views of the Cranberry Islands to the south, western Penobscot Bay and Eagle Lake to the northwest, and Bar Harbor, the Porcupine Islands, and Nova Scotia to the northeast.

But Matt and Jeff's favorite spot, probably because it was off the main trail and they had only discovered it by accident, was Bubble Rock, with an incredible view overlooking Jordan Lake. They had gotten to enjoy the unbelievably romantic spot by themselves for over an hour. And, like at Marblehead Harbor, they now thought of the spot as theirs after leaving something of themselves behind.

All too soon, their two-week stay was over, and it was time to sail home. This time sailing against the wind, the exhilarating close-hauled, tacking-back-and-forth sail home to Swampscott - sighting several humpback whales along the way - took 30 hours.

By then, Jeff was an expert sailor, nearly as good as Matt. As Jeff deftly steered the boat up to the mooring in Swampscott, stopping within easy reach for Matt to pick up the mooring's pennant, Matt smiled and thought, with pride and admiration, "There is nothing this guy can't do."

Jeff was busy with his own thoughts. He was filled with appreciation for all of the experiences Matt had shared with him - from swimming to sailing and now Penobscot Bay - but mostly for the privilege of being his friend. Watching Matt kneel to secure the pennant to the bow cleat, Jeff smiled and thought, "There is nothing I wouldn't do for this guy."

#

PAINT JOB: AUGUST 1945

When Frank greeted Matt and Jeff on their return from Maine, they noticed Frank looked more haggard than usual. Unbeknownst to them, Frank had just started his fourth rapid development jet engine program at General Electric, working on the new J47 axial flow turbojet engine, and the stress on him was beginning to show.

Because of his close association with Sanford Moss and their work on turbochargers, Frank was selected to join the small team of engineers and technicians known as the "Hush-Hush Boys" to work on the secret US jet engine development program at GE at its inception in 1941.

When Whittle secretly visited GE in June 1942, Frank worked closely with him. He even hosted Whittle and brought him home, introducing him to Matt as John Smith, saying he was a visiting engineer from England, engaged in turbocharger work, and would be staying with them for a few days.

Frank was also part of an even smaller sub-group of engineers that, along with Moss, worked with NACA in 1943 on their eight-stage axial flow compressor experiment.

GE's success in quickly developing Whittle's W.1 centrifugal compressor 850 pounds-thrust turbojet design into the 1600 pounds-thrust J31 engine only increased the pressure on the development team. They rapidly developed the follow-on 4000 pounds-thrust centrifugal compressor J33 engine, and then, leveraging their work with NACA, they created the 5600 pounds-thrust axial compressor J35 engine. GE considered the J35 a demonstration engine and now wanted to quickly design a more powerful, fuel-efficient, and robust version: the 5960 pounds-thrust J47 engine, to be used in the USAF's new radically designed jet fighter, the F-86. They had less than two years to do it.

Frank, aware of its importance, had completely invested himself in his work. The result was that for years, he'd let everything else go - his house, yard, car - everything except Matt: nothing was more important to him than Matt.

Without knowing the reason, Matt and Jeff knew Frank was under a lot of pressure at work and had decided together to take some of the load at home off Frank's plate.

They started first with the yard when they returned from Chicago in April. They mowed the lawn, trimmed the hedges, and raked the leaves. Then, they worked on the garden, planting flowers and vegetables when the weather was warmer.

They also started doing all the laundry, house cleaning, food shopping, and cooking. And no matter when Frank got home, there was always a hot meal ready, with Matt and Jeff waiting to have dinner with him: there was no way they would let him eat alone.

At first, Frank was too tired to notice what the boys were up to. But once he did, he thanked them and tried to tell them not to worry, he was fine, and that they should relax and take a break before school started, they deserved it. Matt and Jeff, though, just quietly ignored him.

Now that they were back from Maine, they were anxious to start on their next project: painting the house. They ordered rental scaffolding from a place in Lynn, and when it arrived, they immediately set it up on the side of the house adjacent to the driveway. When Frank got home that night, he was so tired he had trouble processing what the scaffolding was, nearly running into it with his car. When he finally realized what Matt and Jeff were up to, he choked up and could only start, “You don’t have to do this,” before Matt jumped in.

“Dad, it’s no problem. We don’t have anything else to do for the next few weeks, and it’ll keep us busy. Besides, it will give us a chance to work on our tans.

“No worries, OK? Jeff knows all about scaffolding and painting a house safely. His uncle is a house painter, and he taught him when he was a kid. I’m just the grunt labor.”

Jeff added, “Please let us do this, Frank. It’ll be fun for us, and I promise we’ll do a good job.

“We only have one question, Do you want to stay with the same colors, grey with white trim? I think it’s a great combination, but you’ve been living with it for a while and may want to make a change. It won’t take us any longer either way.”

Seeing that they were concerned and wanted to help, Frank relented, but looking at Jeff, teasingly added,

"This won't affect your cooking, I hope. I've gotten pretty spoiled having a great dinner waiting for me when I get home every night."

Jeff smiled and said, "No, we should be good. Besides, you should be asking Matt that question. He's been doing most of the cooking for the past two months. I'm just his technical adviser and dishwasher."

Frank decided to reveal Matt's brush with greatness during dinner, the secret that Matt had met Whittle when he'd stayed with them under an assumed name three years earlier. Whittle had stayed in Matt's room while Matt had sacked out on the couch.

Matt and Jeff now had a glimpse of the importance of Frank's work and vowed that night to take as much of the load off Frank as possible. What they didn't know was they had already eased Frank's mind considerably just through their close friendship: Frank loved seeing them together, so comfortable with each other, and couldn't be happier.

#

BACK TO THE BOOKS AND JOINING THE AIR FORCE ACTIVE RESERVES: FALL 1945

In mid-September, the school term started, and Matt and Jeff became immersed in the engineering-student lifestyle again. Most of their classes were in the Daniel Guggenheim Aeronautical Laboratory building, a wing of the main campus, and just across the street from the Wright Brothers Wind Tunnel building.

The aeronautical engineering 1947 class size was small, and they quickly made friends with students and some of the faculty.

One of their professors learned they were pilots and asked if they would be interested in working part-time as pilots for MIT's Radiation Lab, which had a radar test facility at Hanscom Field, about 10 miles west of Cambridge in Bedford, MA.

Though their initial plan was to try and get a job as technicians at the Wright Brothers Wind Tunnel facility, Matt and Jeff jumped at the chance to earn some extra money flying. They visited the local Civil Aeronautics Authority (CAA) office and, after a review of their military records and taking a competency test, were awarded licenses with multi-engine and instrument ratings.

The Rad Lab had a small fleet of surplus Army and Navy piston engine trainers that were used to test airborne radar systems. Though old, they were well-serviced but weren't the high-performance aircraft Matt and Jeff were used to. Still, they were glad to be flying again.

Soon after they started flying for the Rad Lab, they were approached by a recruiter for the US Army Air Force Reserves about switching their Reserve status from inactive to active. They would be paid for their part-time service, receive the same training as active-duty pilots, and get to fly Hanscom's USAAF Reserve unit's P-51 Mustangs at least 4 hours a month, allowing them to keep their proficiency rating on the Mustang. And they'd be promoted to Captain, to boot!

Again, they jumped at the opportunity and immediately signed up for the Active Reserves. When they told Frank about it later that night at dinner, Frank's initial reaction was negative, but he tried to hide that from them: he thought they'd already given enough. But after considering the idea for a moment, he quickly changed his mind.

He knew the US was repeating the same mistake it had made after WWI when it demobilized too rapidly and released most of its pilots; within five years, few of those pilots were qualified to fly. He could see the same thing was about to happen again: within a year, the USAAF planned to go from having over 150,000 aircraft to having less than 10,000 and would correspondingly reduce its number of pilots.

From his work at GE, he knew the USAAF's plan to make up for their loss in numerical superiority was by having the most technically advanced aircraft. And those aircraft would need pilots with the cutting-edge training to match.

There were already signs the Soviet Union was aggressively pursuing extending its sphere of influence, and the only nation strong enough to counter their aggression was the US.

If a new war started, it could happen quickly, without the lead time the US had before entering WWII. Unlike the Soviet Union, whose forces were still at full strength, the US had demobilized and would have to rely on its active and inactive Reserves to rapidly bring its combat units up to full strength. If that happened, Frank wanted Matt and Jeff to be the best trained, so most valuable pilots in the Reserves, not just one pair out of the hundreds of thousands of Reserve officers called up.

In case he'd let his reticence show, Frank now enthusiastically congratulated them both. He told them that if he seemed initially cool to the idea, it was just that he'd worried for a moment that they might have trouble handling school, work, and the Reserves. But knowing them, he was sure they could do it.

Later that night, though, when he was alone in his room, he shivered from fear and thought, "The Air Force isn't through with them yet. They need to be ready for what's coming."

#

MATCH MAKER: SPRING 1946

Starting in March, to Jeff's annoyance, Matt began playing matchmaker and was constantly introducing Jeff to any girl at school or work he met that he thought was a good fit for Jeff. He'd also not-so-subtly asked the students in their classes if any had a sister their age that was single.

Jeff tried to ignore the problem, but when Matt attempted to fix him up with the assistant librarian as they were checking out books from the Engineering library, Jeff had to confront Matt with it.

"Matt, I know what you're trying to do, so stop it, OK? It's embarrassing.

"We're too busy right now; I'm not looking for anyone else. I'll find someone on my own when I'm ready. I'm happy with the way things are right now. So, knock it off."

Matt thought he'd been pretty slick and that Jeff hadn't noticed his matchmaking. But now that he'd been caught, he thought he'd offer Jeff some encouragement.

"I just want you to be happy. I know you're happy now, but I think you could be even happier.

"Don't worry about me. I'll be fine if you find someone, as long as she's nice and treats you well, is good to you, and you're happy."

Jeff knew this day would come. Matt hadn't backslided once in almost a year. He'd seemed secure to Jeff, like he finally trusted their relationship wouldn't suddenly disappear. Jeff had even been able to go home to Chicago without Matt on Christmas to be with his family and see his brothers, who had recently been discharged, without Matt becoming depressed. But Jeff recognized that Matt's matchmaking was a new form of backsliding, and he wasn't sure how to deal with it.

Jeff hadn't misled Matt. He really wasn't interested in finding a woman to date now. Jeff thought he might in a year or two, but not now. Whoever he found, though, would have to be open-minded and accept his love for Matt. Jeff thought he had enough love in him for two, but if he couldn't find a woman that accepted Matt, he'd stay with Matt.

Jeff, seeing the anguish in Matt's eyes, tried to quickly form a plan.

"Matt, I thought we agreed in Marblehead to give this a rest for a couple of years. I'm very happy right now. I love you. I know you love me. There'll be plenty of time after we graduate for me to find someone to date if I even want to then."

Tears were now pouring from Matt's eyes. He'd felt for a while that he'd been holding Jeff back. He loved Jeff so much; he just wanted him to be happy and was convinced that Jeff couldn't be completely happy unless he had a woman in his life.

Jeff didn't know what else to do, so he pulled Matt into an embrace and offered this.

"You make me very happy; you're wrong if you think you don't. We need to talk to your dad when we get home tonight, though; I need his help. You're hurting, and I don't know what to do. OK?"

When they got home, after dinner, Matt and Jeff asked Frank if they could speak with him.

By the time Jeff had described the problem, Matt was upset again. Surprisingly, though, Frank had a solution to offer.

"Matt, I think you're feeling guilty about keeping Jeff all to yourself, and the happier you are, being alone with Jeff, the guiltier you feel. And the most frightening thing Jeff could say is he's very comfortable being just with you and that he doesn't need anyone else. Am I right?"

Matt could only nod yes.

"Jeff, I think you are very happy being with Matt and don't see the need to change anything right now, if ever. You're frustrated that Matt doesn't believe you, and you're deeply concerned that you're hurting Matt and don't know what to do. I think you're also terrified that if you did start to date someone, even at Matt's instigation, Matt wouldn't be able to handle it and would completely fall apart. Is all this true?"

Jeff, like Matt, just nodded yes.

"So, here's what I think you should do. Jeff, you need to trust Matt that he will be able to handle your dating - and his promise to tell you if he starts to backslide - and start dating some women. Nothing serious at first, just for fun. You could even double-date.

"And Matt, you need to trust Jeff when he tells you that you make him very happy, that you're not holding him back from anything, and his promise that you will be the first to know if things start to become serious when he's dating.

"But you need to let Jeff choose who to date and when, according to his own criteria, and not who you think would be good for him. No more matchmaking. He knows what he's looking for, and he's going to be pretty fussy. So you have to trust him to make the right choice, even if it means he never finds the right person."

All that Matt and Jeff could think was, "Holy crap!" They never dreamed there could be a solution, but somehow Frank had it all figured out. They thanked him and gave him a big hug before going up to bed.

Frank, exhausted from the day's work and his talk with Matt and Jeff, thought before drifting off, "Thank you again, Dr. Spiegel."

In chatting with Frank when he visited, Spiegel had correctly predicted the trajectory of Matt and Jeff's relationship, that Matt, caring so much for Jeff, couldn't be selfish enough to keep Jeff all to himself, and that Jeff cared about Matt so much, he would never consider giving him up.

It wasn't that Spiegel was clairvoyant or a mind reader. In his practice, he had seen similar situations play out, and often successfully, provided those involved in the relationship were honest and upfront with one another. And then he confessed that he was in such a relationship himself.

Two weeks before they were married, Spiegel had told his then-fiancée that he'd had close relationships with men, mostly other psychiatrists, and that, though he loved her deeply, those relationships would likely continue.

She loved him enough to marry him anyway, and they had what he thought was a successful marriage and were raising two boys that he loved more than he could say.

Though a similar situation to Matt and Jeff's, Spiegel said his relationship differed in that his wife was the only woman that he could ever love, but that there were many men he was attracted to, while Jeff was just the opposite: he could love many women, but would only romantically love one man, and that was Matt.

It was an enduring love, though, one that could last a lifetime. But, because it was not in Jeff's general nature to be attracted to men, Matt had a hard time accepting that Jeff wanted him physically and that Jeff denied his true nature by only being with Matt.

What Matt didn't realize was that Jeff now recognized three genders - male, female, and Matt - and that he had as much need to be physically intimate with Matt as Matt had to be with Jeff and that his need wasn't going to fade with time.

Spiegel told Frank he thought Matt and Jeff's relationship would evolve to the point where Matt would start pressing Jeff to date women, thinking it would be the end of their relationship.

If that happened, though, after initially resisting, he thought Jeff would reluctantly agree but then start looking for a woman that would accept his relationship with Matt: that would be one of his most important criteria.

She'd have to be secure and open-minded enough to accept them both into her life, or Jeff wouldn't be seriously interested in her. And she'd have to love Matt, and Matt to love her.

Spiegel thought Jeff was a fine enough catch that he could be selective and find the right woman. And he knew from his own experience there were women like that out there to be found.

#

STEPPIN' OUT

To help build unit camaraderie and to promote recruiting, Hanscom's Reserve commander hosted monthly dances at the base and arranged other social events, like ski trips, on weekends and holidays. Matt and Jeff were usually busy, so they rarely had time to socialize at work or school, but Jeff thought they'd make a special effort and go to that month's dance just to check it out.

The dance was held in the base gymnasium and was well attended. There was a mix of ages, from late teens to early 30s, with about an even number of men and women, unlike the USO dances during the war, which were predominately filled with servicemen.

Matt and Jeff arrived about a half hour after the start of the dance and, after greeting several Reserve members they knew, started mingling in the crowd.

Jeff spotted a group of women that seemed interested in dancing and approached them. He chatted with one of them while keeping his leg in contact with Matt's, then asked her to dance when a fast song was played. They returned to Matt when the song finished, and Jeff, pretending he couldn't hear over the music, put an arm on Matt's shoulder to speak with him.

They moved on to another group, repeating the pattern, and soon Jeff was being noticed by the single women for his dancing.

Jeff was clearly enjoying himself, but though some of the women he danced with seemed interested in him, Jeff didn't return their interest and kept moving on to the next group, never singling anyone out.

Matt enjoyed watching Jeff dance, and though he occasionally felt a pang of jealousy, he mostly felt happy that Jeff was having such a great time. Without realizing it, Matt was learning to trust that Jeff would always come back to him, which was Jeff's plan all along.

They left about an hour before the dance ended, with Jeff tired and sweaty. They were quiet during the ride home. When they got back and were up in their room, Jeff said he was going to take a shower and started to strip. Matt looked away to give him some privacy, but Jeff took that opportunity to move next to Matt and then started undressing him, asking, "Aren't you going to help me wash my back?" before kissing him on the nap of the neck.

For the next few weeks, Jeff noticed how relaxed Matt was. He was back to being his old self and teased and joked with Jeff as he had back at Wormingford, or if they were in a more quiet, intimate mood, like they were in Maine, just comfortable being together.

Jeff really liked the change, so he resolved that they would go to as many of the monthly Reserve dances as possible. By their third dance, they started to be recognized by the regulars, those who came every month, and some women were even comfortable enough to ask Jeff to dance.

One woman, Linda Harrington, a nurse at the base hospital, part of a group of single women that Matt and Jeff often chatted with, had been watching Matt and Jeff closely. She'd kept her distance and never spoken to either of them or been asked to dance by Jeff, but she had been studying them, trying to understand their relationship.

She noticed that Jeff was very attentive to Matt and always made physical contact with him whenever they separated for a few minutes. And Jeff was the more outgoing of the two: Matt was shy, never asked anyone to dance, and only socialized with Jeff.

Then, one time she caught Matt staring a Jeff while he was dancing, with joy on Matt's face from seeing how happy Jeff was, but also, only for a moment, with a touch of sadness. She suddenly thought Matt was wishing it was him that Jeff was dancing with. Jeff might have glanced at Matt at that moment, too, because he made a beeline over to Matt after the dance had finished and put him in a headlock, then tousled his hair, causing Matt to smile.

At the next dance, when Matt and Jeff visited her group, and Jeff had asked one of his 'regulars' to dance, Linda made her way over to Matt. Without pressuring him, she said hello, and, knowing Jeff was probably Matt's favorite subject, remarked how great a dancer Jeff was.

Matt loosened up a little and seemed relaxed as long as they were talking about Jeff. Linda encouraged Matt to keep talking without asking any prying questions and sharing as much information about herself as Matt did about himself and Jeff.

Matt was very interested in her nursing background and that she loved children and worked in the maternity ward. When he asked her what she liked to do for fun, she said she loved to sail and dance. Matt grew quiet. He wasn't sure what to do and didn't want to mislead her, but the next record had started, and it was a slow song. Should he ask her to dance?

Just then, Jeff returned and was amazed to find Matt speaking with someone, especially a woman. But he could tell Matt was distressed because his face was a deep crimson. Thinking he'd try to rescue Matt from an awkward situation, he asked Linda if she wanted to dance. Linda said sure, but maybe the next song; she thought Matt was about to ask her to dance to this one. Then she gently took Matt's hand and led him to the edge of the dance floor.

When they were on the dance floor, Linda wrapped her arms around Matt's neck, while Matt wrapped his around her waist, but Linda kept her body a few inches from Matt's, enough that he was comfortable.

Matt relaxed a little and started to dance, then Linda whispered in his ear, "See, I don't bite. And I can tell from how you're moving Jeff's not the only good male dancer here."

When the song finished, Matt started to lead Linda off the dance floor, but the next song had started, a fast song and one of Jeff's favorites, Tommy Dorsey's hit, "Opus One." Jeff met them and asked Linda to dance. She said sure, but maybe the three of them could dance together. With a huge smile, Jeff said,

"Yes, that sounds great! Come on, Matt, you know this one," and pushed Linda and Matt back onto the floor.

They had a great time dancing together for the next few songs, which were all fast. Then, when a slow song started, Jeff tried to get Linda to dance with him, but she said she wanted to dance one more song with Matt.

Matt, now flustered, concerned Linda was becoming interested in him, went crimson again. But Linda knew the signs and quickly put his mind at ease by asking Matt questions about Jeff. Was he single, what did he like to do, was he a nice guy?

Matt immediately relaxed and started giving Linda all the scoop he could think of on Jeff. It was obvious to Linda now, by how Matt gushed over Jeff, that Matt had a crush on him. But he wasn't possessive of Jeff; he just wanted him to find someone nice.

When she looked at Jeff, she saw the concern on his face, worried Matt was in discomfort. So, she told Matt she had a crush on Jeff, which caused Matt to smile in relief that she wasn't interested in him and that someone as nice as her was interested in Jeff. She glanced at Jeff then and noticed Jeff's concern had changed to relief when he saw Matt smile, convincing her that she'd read their relationship correctly.

When the song finished, a smiling Matt returned with Linda to Jeff, and then when another slow song started, Matt said to Jeff, "I'm tired; it's your turn," and watched as Jeff led Linda onto the dance floor.

Jeff said, "Thanks for being gentle with Matt; he's sometimes a little shy with people."

Linda said, "He's a sweet guy and very fond of you. And you're a good friend, very protective of him. You're lucky to have each other."

Jeff just flat out asked, "Would that bother you, our close friendship? You have no idea what we've been through, how close we are, what we mean to each other?"

Linda said, “I have a brother who was in the Marines. He had a close friend die in his arms at Iwo Jima. I understand more than you think.”

Jeff thought for a moment, then asked, “Was he from Swampscott by any chance?”

Linda, astonished, asked, “Yes, how did you know?”

Jeff said, “Just a guess,” then added, “ But please, promise you’ll never mention it to Matt.”

#

GRADUATION AND BEST MAN: JUNE 1947

Between school, work at the Rad Lab, and training with the Reserves, the following year was busy for Matt and Jeff.

Their classes were demanding but extremely interesting, particularly those covering the emerging science of compressibility and supersonic flow. The Rad Lab had added a C-47 cargo transport, known in civilian aviation as the DC-3, to their fleet, and Matt and Jeff had been checked out and rated to fly it. And their

Reserve unit had received a few P-80 jets, and they were trained on those.

As busy as he was, Jeff always made time for Linda, seeing her at least once a week. Sometimes, they'd only have time for dinner or to grab a quick movie.

By Thanksgiving, things were becoming serious, and Jeff spoke with Matt. He told him he was considering proposing to Linda but only would if Matt approved. Matt told Jeff he loved Linda and thought she'd make the perfect wife for him. So, smiling, Jeff said, "That's good to know because you're going to be my Best Man, or there'll be no wedding."

Jeff proposed to Linda on Christmas Eve, and the two flew to Chicago two days later so Linda could meet Jeff's family.

They timed the wedding to coincide with Graduation in early June so that Jeff's family would only have to make one trip to Massachusetts.

Matt had remained stoic throughout the wedding week, finally meeting Jeff's brothers at the dinner the night before. They immediately lived up to Jeff's description by crashing through Matt's personal space, adopting him as a brother.

He even lived up to his Best Man responsibilities and bucked up a very nervous Jeff just before the ceremony. It wasn't until after he'd handed the ring to Jeff during the wedding that he began to lose control.

They held the reception at the luxurious New Ocean House in Swampscott. Frank and Matt drove together the short distance from the church to the reception. Along the way, Matt started to break down, worried he wouldn't be able to make the toast he'd written to the couple.

Frank gently said, "You'll be able to do it, I know. It's for Jeff, and you'd do anything for him.

"He picked you as his Best Man over any of his four brothers. That's how much you mean to him.

"Nothing's changed, you know; he loves you just the same. Want to know how much? Last night at dinner, he asked me if he should invite you to go along on their honeymoon."

That got Matt to smile. He knew Jeff was just crazy enough to try and arrange it, so Matt thought he'd better buck up a little himself so Jeff didn't get any more bright ideas.

As they were pulling into the hotel's parking lot, Matt said,

"Dad, I've just got to get through this one speech," looking at his written notes, "then I'll be good."

Frank took the notes, a pen from his pocket, and started whittling the speech down, eliminating all but one page and then all but one paragraph on that page.

He handed the notes back and said, "That was a beautiful speech you wrote. I've just edited it a little, down to the essentials. But if you still have any trouble, I'll be right there to deliver it for you. No worries."

After clanging his glass with his knife to get everyone's attention, Matt rose. He raised his glass in a toast and, with eyes brimming, said, "To Jeff, the best and now luckiest Wingman there ever was, and Linda, his equally lucky, beautiful, caring, compassionate, and intelligent wife. May you always have Fair Winds and Following Seas."

When Matt finished and sat down, Frank, who was sitting next to him, put his arm around Matt's shoulder, pulled him into an embrace, then said, "Great job. I don't think I've ever been more proud of you," and continued to hold Matt for a few moments until he sensed he'd recovered his composure a little.

Frank had barely released Matt when all four of Jeff's brothers descended on Matt, back-slapping him, mussing his hair, and congratulating him on making such a great speech. Frank smiled, knowing they were just the thing to cheer Matt up.

They were so much like Jeff, maybe goofier, and there were so many of them that Matt couldn't resist and was soon giggling, doubled over, thanking them for their compliments but begging them to stop their affectionate assault.

They finally stopped after they sensed Matt was no longer feeling sad. They weren't as goofy as they pretended to be and knew what Jeff meant to Matt. They were now as hyper-protective of Matt as they'd always been of Jeff and thought it was cool having two kid brothers.

Jeff had been watching from the other end of the dais and was thankful to have four big brothers as thoughtful and considerate as they were. They'd used that same "bum's rush" trick to cheer Jeff up a million times when he was a kid, and it had always worked.

#

LITTLE GUY AND GODFATHER: MARCH 1948

After graduating, Matt and Jeff continued to work for the Rad Lab, but now full-time.

Jeff and Linda bought an old farm close to Hanscom Field in Concord, MA, just off the old Battle Road used by the Minute Men in 1775. The colonial-era farmhouse was pretty dilapidated, and Jeff and Matt began renovating it in their spare time, preparing it for winter.

By early September, they had made good progress, which was excellent timing, for Linda discovered soon after Labor Day that she was three months pregnant.

In March, Linda delivered a healthy baby boy. Jeff and Linda tried to name the baby after Matt, but he got upset and refused the honor: he thought they should name him either after Jeff or one of their dads. So, they decided to name him Michael after Jeff's dad, but only after Matt agreed to be the godfather.

When Matt held little Mikey during the baptism, he wept through the whole ceremony; his joy was overwhelming. Linda and Jeff were happy, too: they knew they'd never have to worry about finding a babysitter out in the boonies of Concord.

CHAPTER 5 —RETURN TO DUTY: JUNE 1949 - SEPTEMBER 1950

SABRE TRAINING: JUNE 1949

In early June 1949, Matt and Jeff were temporarily assigned to the 59th Fighter Squadron stationed at Otis AFB in Sandwich, MA, on Cape Cod, to satisfy their yearly Air Force Reserve two-week active-duty requirement. There they received training on the USAF's newest, most advanced jet fighter: the F-86A Sabre.

Though much more advanced, Matt and Jeff found transitioning from the 1st-generation P-80 turbojet to the 2nd-generation F-86A reasonably easy. The Sabre required a far shorter runway, was less prone to flame-out, and was significantly more maneuverable. Their only real problem was getting used to the plane's incredible speed.

After their initial 3-day training and a check-out flight, they spent the rest of the Temporary Duty (TDY) assignment flying cross-country training missions, but really, just having fun chasing each other up and down the New England coast.

The Reserve unit at Hanscom wasn't equipped with Sabres yet. So, to keep their proficiency rating on the Sabre active, Matt and Jeff were allotted 4 hours a month to fly the 59th's Sabres at Otis, which could be applied to the Reserve's one-weekend-a-month active-duty requirement as well.

#

RECALLED: 27TH JUNE 1950

In the early morning of Sunday, 25 June 1950, approximately 135,000 North Korean troops crossed the 38th Parallel and began their invasion of South Korea. In response, President Harry S.

Truman ordered the mobilization of the US Reserve Armed Forces to bring the Active Forces up to full strength. Accordingly, reservists that day began to be notified by mail, telegram, and phone to report to their Reserve units for active duty.

The call-up was at first selective, with only the most essential Reserve personnel called. But soon, the call-up was more general, including inactive reservists and draftees, with over 1.5 million men ultimately called to active service.

Matt and Jeff each received a telegram on the 26th of June ordering them to report for duty at Hanscom AFB at 0800 the next day.

Linda drove Jeff to the base while Frank drove Matt. They hugged and said goodbye to their families, and then Matt went to say goodbye to Linda and Jeff to Frank.

Matt hugged and kissed Linda and Mikey, then said, “I don’t know if we’ll be assigned to the same unit, but if we are, I promise to take good care of him. So, no worries, OK?”

Linda said, “I know you will; you always have. He couldn’t have a better Wingman.”

Jeff hugged Frank, and then Frank kissed Jeff on the top of the head.

Jeff said, “If we’re assigned together, I’ll look after him and keep you posted, like before.”

Frank said, “I know you will; he couldn’t have a better friend. Just promise you’ll take care of yourself, too. I love you like a son.”

Jeff said he would, then added, “That’s quite the gizmo you and GE designed. You’ve given us the best chance to win in a dogfight. Is that why you changed your mind a few years back when Matt and I joined the Reserves? You wanted us to be well-trained on the best aircraft?”

Frank paused – he was always amazed despite Jeff’s easy-going exterior, how perceptive he was - then somberly said,

“Yes. I was worried you’d be recalled and stuck in either a meat grinder war-of-attrition, fighting on the ground, or flying some obsolete WWII-era prop job salvaged from the moth-ball air fleet. I thought the Air Force would be careful how they deployed their prime asset, and if you two were flying their best fighter, they'd be careful how they deployed you as well."

Then Frank added, "The Sabre is a great plane, and I think it has the best jet engine in the world: we still have a slight edge with jets. But don't get cocky and lulled into the Air Force brass's idea that the Sabre is so superior that it'll always dominate the skies. There are rumors of a Russian plane that can give it a run for its money. You'll still have a good chance of winning in combat if you respect your opponent and work as a team. You Air Force guys are the best-trained pilots in the world, and that's always been a huge advantage."

#

4TH FIGHTER-INTERCEPTOR GROUP: JUNE – SEPTEMBER 1950

To their immense relief, the USAF assigned Matt and Jeff to the same Active Air Force unit, the 4th Fighter-Interceptor Group, 335th Fighter-Interceptor Squadron, equipped with F-86A Sabres and stationed at Langley AFB in Hampton, Virginia.

The same morning Matt and Jeff were activated, they were flown from Hanscom to Langley and arrived just in time to join their squadron, leaving for Advanced Gunnery training at Nellis AFB, Las Vegas, Nevada.

Most of the pilots in the squadron were younger, lower-ranking officers and had never seen combat. They were affable, though, and impressed by Matt and Jeff's war experience, welcomed them to the unit. There was friendly competition between the younger and older pilots on the gunnery range, with the more senior pilots losing slightly but still holding their own.

After the two-week training, the squadron returned to Langley and resumed its Air Defense Command duties, defending the air space over the US mid-Atlantic East Coast region.

Matt and Jeff quickly accumulated over 200 flight hours in the Sabre, bringing them up to par with the rest of the squadron.

In September, the Group, now assigned to the newly-formed Eastern Air Defense Force, part of the 26th Air Division, moved to the nearly-abandoned, WWII-era Dover AFB in Wilmington, Delaware. The hangars and housing facilities were rundown, and everyone, officers and enlisted men alike, quickly worked to make the base functional and livable. Initially, however, the Group was housed in tents, which, as it turns out, was good practice for what was soon to come.

CHAPTER 6— KOREA: DECEMBER 1950 – JANUARY 1952

DEPLOYMENT TO SOUTH KOREA: NOVEMBER 1950

On 1 November 1950, a flight of F-51 Mustangs and B-26 Marauder bombers attacking an airfield near Sinuiju, North Korea, just across the Yalu River from the border with China, were jumped by six swept-wing jet fighters. The USAF aircraft managed to escape and reported that Russian-built MiG-15s had entered the Korean conflict.

Within days, the Chinese-based MiGs attacked formations of B-29s that were bombing bridges crossing the Yalu River. Though F-80 Shooting Star jet fighters were escorting the bombers, the MiGs were 100 mph faster, and the escorts were too slow to provide adequate protection; one B-29 was lost. When three B-29s were shot down on a single mission a few days later, the USAF temporarily halted its daylight strategic bombing campaign.

To counter the MiG threat, on 9 November 1950, the USAF ordered the 4th Fighter-Interceptor Group to deploy immediately to Kimpo AB, South Korea.

Before flying to their West Coast embarkation points, the Group first exchanged their older '48 model F-86A Sabres for the best "low time" F-86As available from other Sabre units. Then, the 334th and 335th Squadrons flew to San Diego, where their planes were loaded aboard a Navy escort carrier, while the 336th flew to San Francisco, where their Sabres were loaded aboard tankers.

The ground crews and technical representatives accompanied the airplanes, but the pilots were flown to Johnson AB, Japan, from Travis AFB, CA, by way of Midway Atoll, aboard C-54 transports.

The 336th Squadron's planes arrived in Japan first, on 26 November, and were quickly serviced and inspected. As soon as the first seven aircraft of the Squadron's total of 25 were ready, this sub-group, called Detachment A, flew to Kimpo AB, South Korea, USAF designation K-14, arriving on 13 December 1950.

This small detachment of Sabres was almost immediately thrown into the air battle against the MiGs. They flew their first mission on 15 December and then scored their first MiG victory on 17 December, quickly demonstrating that the Sabre was a match for the MiG.

Unfortunately, the ground war was going badly for the UN forces. By the end of December, the North Korean forces were advancing on the nearby South Korean capital of Seoul, and on 2 January 1951, the 336th was ordered to evacuate Kimpo and return to Japan.

Though they had only been in combat a little over two weeks, the Sabres had scored eight MiG victories versus one loss for a kill ratio of 8:1 and regained control of the air space. As importantly, they had confirmed that the limited range of the MiGs restricted their operations to a small region in the northwestern corner of North Korea along the Yalu River bordering China, now named by the UN pilots MiG Alley.

Matt and Jeff arrived with the rest of the pilots of the 335th Squadron at Johnson AB on 28 November 1950. The 334th and 335th Squadron's aircraft didn't arrive in Japan until 10 December, two weeks after the 336th's, so none of their pilots were part of Detachment A, the first Sabre pilots deployed to Korea.

Johnson AB, a former Japanese pilot training air base located just north of Tokyo, was heavily bombed during WWII but had been fully rebuilt by the USAAF when they occupied it after the war. The runways had been extended, new hangars built, and Quonset huts added, providing housing for personnel, administration buildings, and medical facilities. The base became a major USAAF facility, headquarters to the Fifth Air Force. More permanent buildings were built, and by December of 1950, the base was headquarters for several USAF Far East Air Force command units, including the 4th Fighter-Interceptor Wing and the 3rd Bombardment Wing.

The 335th's pilots spent the first six weeks in Japan helping the maintenance crews offload, inspect, and repair the Sabres: all the planes had suffered some degree of galvanic corrosion damage from exposure to seawater. They also brought the aircraft and their records up to date, preparing them for combat.

With the evacuation of Detachment A from Korea, the Sabres saw little combat for the first two weeks in January 1951: the operating radius of the F-86As was only 500 miles, putting them out of range of MiG Alley, which was 800 miles from Johnson.

By mid-January, the Chinese ground offensive had been slowed. As a result, the decision was made to return a small advance group of Sabres to Korea, operating from Taegu AB, designated K-2, located in the southeastern corner of South Korea and one of the only airfields still in UN control.

Matt and Jeff were selected to be part of Detachment B, a group of eight Sabre pilots from the 335th Squadron.

Detachment B arrived at Taegu AB on 14 January. The base was still out of range of MiG Alley, but the group began flying two-armed reconnaissance missions a day, armed with 5-inch HVAR rockets and bombs. They flew under the control of the T-6 Mosquito Squadron, which was flying forward air control over the front lines.

The conditions at K-2 were horrible, especially for flying advanced jet aircraft. The taxiways and runways were pierced steel plank (PSP) that did a number on the Sabre's high-pressure tires. There were no hangars, and the Sabres were serviced on the open ramps, often in -40 F weather.

Living quarters were primitive. Matt and Jeff found themselves sharing an eight-man tent with the rest of the Detachment's pilots. The tent had a wooden floor, and they slept in sleeping bags on canvas cots. There were two potbellied oil-fueled stoves for heat, but there was no running water: they used a metal combat helmet turned upside-down on a plywood table as a common sink.

The lavatory facilities were even cruder, consisting of an outhouse tent with a long plank supported by several 55-gallon drums, with a hole cut above each drum. Everyone learned to hold their breath and quickly do their business

There was another tent for weekly group showers. The lukewarm water was initially turned on for a moment to let the group get wet, then shut off while they lathered, before being briefly turned on again while they rinsed.

A perimeter fence, patrolled 24 hours a day by armed guards, surrounded the base to keep infiltrators out. Still, everyone slept fully clothed with a loaded pistol under their pillow.

The Mess Hall was the one bright spot. The food was served by Korean houseboys and was excellent, prepared by a cook rumored to have been a chef at an upscale New York restaurant before the war.

On 22 February 1951, elements of the 334th Squadron relieved Detachment B, who, now designated Detachment C, were ordered to Niigata AB, Japan, to provide air defense to counter the rising threat of potential Chinese and Russian bomber attacks on USAF bases in Japan from Vladivostok.

The UN ground war continued to improve, and Suwon AB, designated K-13, about 23 miles south of Seoul, was recaptured. By 10 March, the base had been rebuilt and was ready for full operations, and all of the 334th Squadron's Sabres were deployed there. The 334th's F-86As could now reach MiG Alley, and they began flying twice-daily patrol missions to the area.

On 1 May 1951, after flying 1073 sorties and scoring 16 MiG victories, the 334th Squadron was relieved by the 335th. The 334th then returned to Johnson AB for a well-deserved period of rest and relaxation (R&R).

#

MIG FEVER

Matt and Jeff, and the rest of Detachment C rejoined the 335th Squadron at Johnson AB just before its deployment to Suwon.

The eight Detachment pilots were all WWII veterans and had been selected to be the first from their squadron to be placed in combat because of their prior war experience.

But being older and more experienced in combat and then separated from the squadron for almost five months had isolated the Detachment's members from the rest of the squadron, where clicks had formed among its younger pilots.

Once they'd arrived at Suwon and started flying missions to MiG Alley, Matt and Jeff noticed other changes.

There was an aggressiveness in the younger pilots, encouraged by their commanders, that violated the ethos that had been ingrained in the WWII veterans. The concepts of mutual support and never leaving your wingman behind were replaced by the selfish pursuit of scoring MiG kills at all costs to achieve the notoriety of Ace status.

Violation of the UN rule of not crossing the Yalu by pilots was commonplace, and instead of resulting in a reprimand, it was rewarded by commanders.

What became known as MiG Madness affected almost everyone, including commanders. One squadron commander's aggressiveness, combined with poor eyesight, resulted in his firing on three members of his own flight. Another flight leader, trying to become a double Ace, shot down his wingman.

To stay on station longer in MiG Alley, many pilots flew past Bingo Fuel, where they had just enough fuel to make it back to base safely. To get home, they'd climb to high-altitude, shut the engine off, then glide most of the way back to base. If, when they were on final approach, the engine wouldn't start, or they'd run too low on fuel, they'd have to make a dead-stick landing. Several pilots died attempting this risky practice.

Matt and Jeff, as flight leaders, soon scored one MiG victory each. But since their flights had never crossed the Yalu, they were judged by the squadron commander, Lieutenant Colonel

Benjamin H. Emmet, as not aggressive enough and were replaced with younger pilots of the same rank with more kills but less time-in-grade, the new standard being merit over experience. They were both reduced to wingmen and assigned to different flights – Matt to Red flight and Jeff to Blue – and were billeted separately in their assigned flight's tent.

#

MISSION: TOP AIR COVER OVER MIG ALLEY: 26 JULY 1951

The 335th's mission for the day was to fly north to the Yalu River and provide top air cover for F-84s and F-80s from the 49th Fighter-Bomber Wing against any MiG-15 fighters crossing the river. The fighter-bombers would engage in interdiction raids over North Korean bridges, roads, and railways along the south side of the Yalu, from the Changjin Reservoir west to Sinuiju at the mouth of the Yalu River.

The Squadron's group of four flights, designated Red, White, Blue, and Green, each with four Sabres for a total of 16 F-86As, would be commanded by Major John Dodd, leader of Blue Flight.

The patrol altitude would be 35,000 feet, and Bingo fuel was set at 250 gallons, allowing for a 25-minute patrol. Takeoff would be at 1400, arrival over the patrol area at 1427, departure from the patrol area at 1452, and return to base at 1519. The forecast for takeoff, landing, and the patrol area was for good weather, with light to moderate winds from the south and clear skies.

After the briefing, Matt and Jeff checked their assignments on the mission board. As they had for several weeks, Jeff was flying Flight Wingman, callsign Blue 2, behind Blue Flight Leader, Major Dodd, callsign Blue 1. And Matt was flying Flight Wingman, callsign Red 2, behind Red Flight Leader, Captain Paul Jenkins, callsign Red 1.

The mission proceeded without incident until the squadron reached the patrol area near Sinuiju. There, Major Dodd spotted a wave of approximately 70 MiGs at 40,000 feet on the north side of the Yalu, flying parallel to the Sabres. Dodd radioed, "Many MiGs crossing. Drop tanks and engage," a command to break down into two ship-element pairs and attack.

Dodd immediately dove to chase a MiG at his one o'clock position that had overshot a Sabre. He radioed Jeff, "Stay with me, Blue Two," as they chased the MiG from 30,000 feet down to the deck. The Major scored several solid hits before the MiG crossed the river into forbidden territory, trying to escape.

But Dodd had no intention of letting the MiG go. He followed the MiG across the river and down a runway of the nearby Chinese airfield at Antung, with Jeff close behind, covering Dodd's left side from any MiGs looking to join the fight.

Dodd continued to score hits, eventually blowing the canopy off the MiG, which was flying so low its jet exhaust created plumes of dust from the ground.

The Major chased the MiG between two hangars at over 300 knots before firing several rounds that hit the MiG's port wing, breaking it off and causing the MiG to instantly crash into the ground in a field beside the runway.

Dodd immediately started a zoom-climb to regain altitude with Jeff close behind when Jeff's plane was hit by flak from one of the air base's many radar-directed anti-aircraft guns. Smoke, fuel, and hydraulic fluid began spewing from the belly of the Sabre. Jeff radioed,

"Blue 2 to Blue 1. I've been hit. Leaking fuel badly."

Dodd, though, had his blood up and, after just getting his fifth MiG and becoming an Ace, was obsessed with scoring another kill. He radioed Jeff,

"Roger, Blue 2. Looks like you're well past Bingo, so return to base. I'm going to hunt solo here for a bit longer. Good luck."

Jeff, disappointed but not surprised to be abandoned by the Major, didn't bother to acknowledge the message.

Jeff's first concern was to gain as much altitude as possible before all his fuel leaked out. He knew the Air Force had a helicopter rescue detachment at Cho Do Island in the Yellow Sea just off the North Korean mainland about 107 miles southeast of Antung, which was at the limit of the Best Glide distance of the Sabre from 40,000 feet.

Warning lights were flashing, and alarms were sounding as every system on the Sabre began shutting down. Just as the Sabre reached 28,500 feet, the engine flamed out, and Jeff pointed the nose over, trying to maintain the Best Glide speed of 185 knots, and following the radio compass indicator's heading to Cho Do Island, but now knowing that he'd likely fall short by 30 miles.

He switched the AN/APX-6 Identify Friend or Foe (IFF) transponder, which sent a uniquely-coded radar signal for Ground Control to track individual friendly aircraft, from normal Mode 3 to emergency Mode 4, hoping the rescue detachment at Cho Do would be notified. Then he reviewed his checklist for ejecting and prepared his aircrew flight equipment for survival at sea.

#

NUDGE AT 8000 FEET

Matt had just finished providing cover for Captain Jenkins while he scored a MiG kill when Matt heard Jeff's radio message saying he'd been hit. With the sky clear of MiGs and the fighter-bombers on their way back to base, Matt radioed,

"Red 2 to Red 1, I'm past Bingo and heading back to base," receiving, "Roger Red 2," in response. Then Matt radioed Combat Operations and asked for a vector heading to intercept Jeff.

Due to the additional drag from the battle damage, Jeff was having trouble achieving the Sabre's maximum glide ratio of about 2.5 miles traveled per 1000 feet of altitude lost. In fact, it looked like he was barely meeting half that value, which meant he'd likely only make it halfway to Cho Do. He'd already lost 15,000 feet and had only traveled about 20 miles, with 87 miles to go and only 13,500 feet of altitude remaining. There was no way the rescue helicopter could reach him, so his only chance was for a seaplane to rescue him. But when he glanced at the sea below, he thought it looked too rough for that.

Just then, he heard Matt trying to raise him on the radio.

"Red 2 to Blue 2. Over."

Matt was closing on Jeff quickly. He could see the extensive damage to the plane and was surprised Jeff could keep it in the air. He decided not to mention that, though.

As Matt used his speed brakes to slow, then idled his engine and pulled along Jeff's port side, Jeff waved and said,

"Blue 2 to Red 2, glad to see you. Over."

Matt waved back and, with concern, asked,

"What's your status, Blue 2? How are you doing? Are you injured?"

Jeff answered that he wasn't injured, then described his high rate of descent, that he wasn't going to make Cho Do, and that he was too far offshore to try for the mainland.

They were both silent for a moment as they fell below 10,000 feet. Jeff knew he'd have to eject soon or risk impact injury, and ditching wasn't an option in rough seas.

Jeff finally broke the silence. Looking at Matt, with his hand pressed to the inside of the canopy, as close to Matt as he could get, he said,

"Promise you'll take care of them."

Matt, also with his hand pressed to the inside of the canopy, said, "I promise."

Jeff said, "I'm going to eject at 5000 feet. You'll have to pull away before I do. I don't want to risk something flying off and bringing you down with me." Then he added, "You've been the best friend there ever was, the best thing that's ever happened to me."

As they passed below 8000 feet, a little angry, Matt said, "The hell with this! Do you trust me?"

Jeff said, "Yes, but I'm not going to let you do anything stupid."

Matt said, “You’re always telling me how great a pilot I am. Did you really mean it, or was it just a lot of hot air?”

Jeff said, “No, I meant it. You’re the best pilot I've ever met.”

Matt said, “Well, let’s prove it. Give me 30 seconds flying straight and level at 150 knots. Oh, and definitely don’t try to restart your engine.”

Jeff asked, “Why, what are you going to do?”

Matt said, “I’m going to give you a little nudge to Cho Do.”

Jeff said, “That’s crazy. You can’t do that.”

Matt replied, “Maybe crazy for anybody else, but not for the greatest pilot in the world.

“Look, if I’m half the pilot you say I am, this should work. But you have to be on your game, too. You have the hardest part: keeping that wreck of a plane straight and level flying a dead-stick ship. We’re losing altitude. Are you game or not?”

Jeff said, “If you say you can do it, I believe you.”

Matt said, “Good. Now, do whatever you have to do to give me 30 seconds of straight and level at 150 while I loop around. When you think you’re set, let me know, and I’ll make my approach. This should be a piece of cake.”

With that, Matt fell back, then increased the engine throttle to full. He dove to gain speed and distance from Jeff, then looped around, ending up loitering about 500 feet behind Jeff.

Jeff pulled straight and level but found his speed bled off too fast to last 30 seconds at 150 knots. So, he put the plane in a steeper dive to gain more speed, then leveled off, radioing Matt he should approach.

Matt leveled and centered his plane with Jeff’s and slowly approached, using a combination of throttle and speed brakes. When he was positioned inches from Jeff’s exhaust and flying at the same speed as Jeff, Matt retracted the speed brakes as he increased the throttle, and the two planes docked with a slight jolt.

Matt continued to increase the throttle. Both planes remained docked and began to accelerate. When they reached 190 knots, the planes started to buffet, so Matt reduced the throttle slightly to find the optimum, buffet-free setting.

Jeff was beside himself. “Holy crap! We are the greatest pilots in the world.”

Matt, smiling, said, “Hey, don’t get conceited. We still have 60 miles to go.” They could see Cho Do Island, now about 10 minutes away.

As they approached the island, Matt confirmed with Jeff that he’d reviewed his ejection checklist, then they fell silent.

When Jeff started to thank Matt, he cut him off, saying,

“You can buy me a beer tonight when you get back. I’ll be waiting for you. I hope you remember all your swimming lessons.”

Jeff said, “It’s a deal,” then, “No worries, I remember them all, but especially my instructor.”

Matt said, “I hope the speed brakes undock us, or I’ll be ejecting with you.”

Matt idled the engine, then partially deployed the speed brakes, smoothly separating the two planes.

Then just before Jeff ejected, Matt said, “Good luck, Jeff,” and moved his plane a safe distance away.

A moment later, Jeff’s canopy flew off, and Jeff was catapulted out of the cockpit. Matt watched as Jeff’s ejector seat fell away and his parachute opened. At the same time, Matt saw the rescue helicopter rise and head in Jeff’s direction.

Matt would have liked to stay to watch the rescue to be sure Jeff was safe, but he was almost out of fuel and needed to reach 30,000 feet before his fuel ran out: he was the one now who would have to glide back to the field and make a dead-stick landing.

#

MED EVACUATED

After notifying the Control Tower, who briefly shut the field down, Matt landed safely. He was met by his crew chief, Staff Sergeant (SSgt) Warren Holbrook, and apologized for the damage to the plane’s nose.

At first, when Matt explained how the damage happened, SSgt Holbrook didn't believe him. But a few minutes later, when the radio traffic between Matt and Jeff leaked out, he and the rest of the ground crew were in awe. Then SSgt Holbrook told Matt not to worry about the damage; the mechanics had a plane they cannibalized parts from that had a perfect nose, the repair was a simple one, and Matt's plane would be as good as new within three hours.

After debriefing, Matt made his way over to the Air Rescue area to see if there was any word on Jeff. There he learned that Jeff had been seriously injured when he'd ejected: his leg had caught on something and been badly broken. They were flying him in by helicopter now, and once he was stabilized, he would be Medical Evacuated to Japan for surgery.

Matt was beside himself with grief. It all seemed surreal; he and Jeff had been celebrating in the air just an hour earlier.

Matt waited by the Med Evac area, and about an hour later, he heard a helicopter approaching. When the helicopter had landed, they removed the external pod holding Jeff and opened it.

Jeff was wrapped in a blanket but was still shivering from the cold. They had given him a shot to sedate him, so he wasn't really with it. But when he saw Matt, he started screaming,

"They're going to take my leg! Matt, don't let them take my leg!"

Matt didn't know what to do. They took Jeff into the Med Evac tent and started prepping him for the flight to Japan. Matt saw a doctor and asked if they planned to remove Jeff's leg.

The doctor told him Jeff's lower right leg was shattered, and they didn't think they could save it. But he was pretty sure they could keep just below the knee, which would make a big difference.

Matt begged. Wasn't there any chance of saving the leg? Seeing the devastation on Matt's face, the doctor offered this.

"There is an orthopedic surgeon in Japan, probably the best in the world. If anyone can save the leg, he can. But the recovery will be more difficult and painful and require multiple surgeries. Do you think Jeff is prepared for that? He could go through all that pain and still lose the leg."

Matt said, "Yes. If there is any chance to save the leg, Jeff wants to take it."

The doctor said fine; he'd let the doctors in Japan know.

They were getting ready to load Jeff onto the Med Evac plane. Matt only had a minute to speak to him.

"Jeff, I spoke with the doctor. There's an expert in Japan, and they will do everything they can to save your leg. But if it's a no-go, you have to accept it. If they save your leg, the recovery won't be easy, and you'll have to do everything they tell you to do, even though it's painful."

Desperately fighting to keep from crying, Matt said,

"You keep telling me I have a magic touch, and I keep saying that I don't.

"Well, I lied, I do," as Matt touched the thigh of Jeff's injured leg. "I'm touching you now, and I promise your leg will feel better soon."

Suddenly lucid for a moment, Jeff stared into Matt's eyes and said,

"Thanks, it feels better already."

Then Matt reached into his pocket and pulled out his medallion, and placed it in Jeff's hands, saying,

"This is the source of all my magic; it will bring you luck, too. Keep it for me until I see you again back home."

At that moment, the orderlies lifted Jeff's stretcher, and Matt waved goodbye as they loaded Jeff onto the plane.

Matt waited for the Med Evac plane to climb out of sight before walking the short distance to the makeshift Officer's Club.

There he found Major Dodd celebrating his newly acquired Ace status with a cadre of officers from the Squadron. Matt walked up to the Major, hauled off, and punched him squarely on the jaw, knocking him to the floor.

The Major, a blackbelt in judo, had been caught off-guard. He ordered two lieutenants to hold Matt. Then he delivered a roundhouse kick to Matt's chest, cracking three of his ribs.

Dodd was winding up to deliver another blow when the Squadron Operations Officer, Major Frederick Blesse, on loan from the 334th, aimed his revolver at Dodd's head and said,

"Don't try to kick him again, or I might have an accidental discharge." Blesse had been in Command Operations, heard the radio traffic between Matt and Jeff, and followed Matt, who he'd noticed walking with determined purpose, into the Officer's Club.

Then Blesse gave Dodd some more advice.

"You've gotten your Ace; now I think it's time for you to leave Korea.

"I want you off the base within three hours. If not, I'll tell those reporters outside waiting to fawn all over you how you left your wingman behind today, unprotected in a crippled ship, to hunt MiGs. And how you shot your own wingman down a month ago, despite his frantic calls telling you that you were firing at him. He's a POW now, probably being tortured as we speak."

Then Major Blesse put an arm around Matt's shoulder and helped him to the medical tent.

That night, Major Dodd quietly left for Japan on rotation back to the US. The next day, after word of Matt's heroic push to save Jeff spread, Matt was promoted to Major. He was also made the new leader of Blue Flight.

****

Major Frederick "Boots" Blesse became a legend in the Korean theater of war. Upon arriving for his second tour, he saw how deplorable the state of flight leadership in the squadrons had become. He is credited with reviving the WWII principle of mutual support before, during, and after engagement. He developed the fighting wing formation and implemented the shooter-cover-roles concept, which together, again made the formation a mutually supportive team in which every pilot played an important role. He did all this while also becoming an Ace himself.

Reemphasizing the ethos of flight leadership resulted in a marked decrease in fighter pilot attrition with a corresponding increase in kill ratios. Though not solely attributable to improvements in flight leadership, during the last months of the war, the 4th Fighter-Interceptor Group managed to achieve kill ratios as high as 50:1 over the MiGs, one of the reasons that finally forced the North Koreans back to the peace table.

#

WORKING FOR EARLY ROTATION: AUGUST 1951 – JANUARY 1952

Sensing that Jeff would need him, Matt did everything he could to get rotated home as soon as possible.

The rules for pilot rotation had recently changed. To be eligible for rotation, a pilot had to serve in combat for one year and flown at least 100 missions. The kicker, though, was the Air Force gave priority to rotating married pilots first, especially those with children.

Matt would satisfy the one-year-in-combat requirement by December and thought he could offset being unmarried by flying many more than the required 100 missions. So, he volunteered to fly as many missions as possible, declining an offer in September for a two-week stay in Japan for some R&R.

Matt's goal was to be home by Christmas, but he thought there might be too many married pilots competing for that time of year. He'd settle for mid-January. But if worse came to worst, he would complete his 20-month maximum active-duty service obligation by the end of February unless Congress passed a proposed law to extend it indefinitely. He decided that if that happened, he'd resign his commission: he was hellbent on being home no later than the beginning of March.

Flying nearly every day, as often as the weather permitted, Matt quickly surpassed the 100-mission requirement. He also accumulated more victories and, by October, had become an Ace.

By late December, he'd flown over 150 missions and scored eight victories. In mid-January 1952, he finally received orders to be rotated home. With luck, he'd be back in the US by the end of the month.

CHAPTER 7 – AGONY: JULY 1951 – FEBRUARY 1952

MEDICAL DISCHARGE: JULY – SEPTEMBER 1951

Jeff received the best of care in the Air Force hospital in Japan. His orthopedic surgeon, a draftee like 99% of the doctors and nurses who served during the Korean War, lived up to his reputation and managed to save Jeff's leg. But the operation had been difficult and used many surgical metal implants that would require multiple surgeries to remove months later once the bones had healed.

Two weeks after his surgery, Jeff was airlifted back to the US. Again, his treatment at the Air Force Medical Service (AFMS) hospital at Travis AFB, CA, was excellent. There was no sign of infection, and his pain seemed to be lessening.

But because his prognosis was for decreased mobility, his flying status was changed to inactive. He was then determined to be medically unfit for duty and received a medical discharge from the Air Force with a 25% disability.

He was flown to Hanscom AFB, where he was met by an ambulance and transported to the Veterans Administration (VA) hospital in West Roxbury, MA.

Linda visited the same day he was admitted, and they embraced, with Jeff standing on crutches during their tearful but joyful reunion.

#

VETERANS ADMINISTRATION NEGLECT: OCTOBER 1951

Jeff soon noticed a significant decrease in the quality of care between his treatment in the Air Force and the VA hospitals.

Though the doctors and nurses were well trained, the VA hospital was drastically understaffed and underfunded for the volume of patients it received. The staff was overwhelmed, with the result that a triage system was implemented, with only critical care provided. Those patients requiring convalescent or rehabilitation care were essentially ignored, just warehoused.

Forced to juggle too many patients, the doctors resorted to over-prescribing pain medications, and the nurses neglected patient hygiene, leaving the patients in an unhealthy, zombie-like state.

Linda noticed Jeff's quick decline and, after unsuccessfully trying to advocate for better in-hospital care, requested outpatient care for Jeff: she knew she could give him better treatment herself at home.

The VA, happy to reduce its patient burden by one, obliged and released Jeff after arranging in-home bi-weekly visits from a physical therapist and providing a copious amount of prescription pain medication.

#

HOME TO CONCORD AND DOWNWARD SPIRAL: NOVEMBER 1951 - JANUARY 1952

When Jeff arrived home, he broke down and wept: he was so happy to be home and out of the VA hospital.

Linda had left Mikey with the babysitter, a neighbor who was a retired school teacher. But before she picked him up, she wanted to make Jeff presentable.

Jeff was able to move around pretty well on his crutches, and she shepherded him into the first-floor bathroom. She ran the water into the tub and started undressing Jeff. When Jeff tried to undress her, she said,

"Whoa, cowboy, not now. I just want to get you clean and then go get Mikey."

Jeff said, "Well, it's been a while, and I've missed you so much. I don't know if a certain part of me will behave."

Smiling, Linda said, "Well, no worries if it doesn't. I'm sure we can get it to misbehave again once we put Mikey to bed," then passionately kissed Jeff on the lips. She'd missed Jeff just as much and was aching to be held by him.

For the next two days, Jeff was very happy and pain-free, enough so that Linda was able to wean him off the pain medication.

But on the third day, the physical therapist arrived, and things took a dramatic turn for the worse.

The therapist, an arrogant, muscled man in his late 30s, had ignored Jeff's screams of pain when he tried stretching Jeff's injured leg too far. The session left Jeff in excruciating pain, which left Linda with little choice but to give Jeff more pain medication.

When his pain persisted the next day, Linda took Jeff back to the VA hospital. The doctor there said Jeff had to accept pain as part of his physical therapy. Linda, though, no longer trusted the VA and didn't believe anything the doctor had told them.

The next day, Linda spoke to one of the doctors at work. He told her a small amount of pain was to be expected but that the amount of pain Jeff was experiencing was excessive and indicated something was seriously wrong. The pain could indicate an infection, or the hardware installed during the surgery might have failed. To be sure, he'd need to look at some x-rays of the leg, but it would be better if Jeff saw a specialist. He then mentioned that complicated reconstruction surgery like that performed on Jeff always required follow-up surgeries and asked if the VA had scheduled any surgery yet.

Linda, now desperate, tried to get Jeff to go with her to see a private orthopedic surgeon. But Jeff, not having any insurance, refused. So, Linda went back to the VA and asked when they planned on scheduling the subsequent surgeries, but they were non-committal: the VA was more overwhelmed than ever and wanted to delay what they considered elective surgery for as long as possible.

Meanwhile, Jeff was in constant agony and became increasingly addicted to the pain medication. The medication was becoming less effective, though, so he started self-medicating with alcohol.

When the physical therapist showed up again, six weeks late, for another session, Linda chased him away at the point of a kitchen knife.

By then, Jeff's demeanor had considerably changed. He'd stopped eating regularly and become verbally abusive to Linda. She thought, "He's trying to drive me away."

She noticed that the only joy remaining in Jeff's life was Mikey. No matter how much pain he was in, he was always kind and loving toward Mikey.

CHAPTER 8 — HOME: JANUARY - FEBRUARY 1952

BEST ACTOR AWARD: 29 JANUARY 1952

The moment Matt got off the plane at Travis AFB, CA, at 0800 that Tuesday morning when he arrived back in the US from Korea, he called Jeff.

When Jeff answered the phone and recognized Matt's voice, he was beside himself. For the first time in months, he felt real joy. His depression temporarily vanished, and he started bantering with Matt, then in rapid succession, asked Matt how he was and what his plans were.

Matt was trying to get a word in edgewise, desperate to learn how Jeff was doing. But Jeff was being evasive and always turned the conversation back to learning about Matt.

Matt sensed something was off and asked to speak with Linda, saying he just wanted to say hello. When Linda took the phone, she tried to continue Jeff's upbeat conversation, but Matt stopped her.

"Hi, Linda. I'm really glad to hear your voice again, but I can tell something is wrong. If that's true, say, "OK."

Linda, still smiling, said, "OK."

Matt's heart sank. He'd guessed in Korea that something was wrong. He'd written Jeff a letter every week but never gotten a reply. Now he knew why.

"Linda, I know you can't talk now. As soon as you can, get to a pay phone and call my dad. He'll have a number where you can reach me. I'll be there, waiting by the phone, for your call. I promise everything will be better soon. Now, give me back to Jeff so he doesn't suspect something's up."

Linda handed the phone back to Jeff and listened to Jeff's side of the conversation until Matt ended the call.

After a few minutes, Linda said she needed to go to the store and would be back in half an hour or so. Jeff, still smiling, said OK, no worries, he and Mikey would be fine.

#

DESPERATE CALLS

About twenty minutes later, Linda called Matt, reversing the charges as Matt's dad had instructed. Matt answered,

"Hi, Linda. Just so you're not worried, I'm in a special phone booth on the base provided for guys to call home. I'll pay for the call when we finish. There's no time pressure; we can talk for as long as we want. I don't have to waste time putting coins in every three minutes, and we won't be interrupted by the operator. OK?"

Relieved, Linda said she understood. Then Matt asked her to describe everything that was happening with Jeff.

She described the neglect at the VA, Jeff's abuse by the physical therapist, his excruciating pain resulting from it, and his growing addiction to pain meds. Then she went further, describing Jeff's depression from other problems he faced that were not medically related.

They were struggling financially, and Jeff was worried the bank was about to repossess the car and foreclose on the farm. But he knew he wasn't physically able to hold a job.

Jeff was convinced he'd never fly or dance again, two things that mattered most to his self-esteem. And then Linda paused, unsure if she should share Jeff's most intimate problem.

Matt sensed Linda's reluctance to go further and said,

"Linda, Jeff and I have no secrets from each other. We've both seen each other at rock bottom. He knows personal secrets about me that I thought I could never share. And he can read me like a book; it's scary sometimes not being able to hide my feelings from him. But I know I can trust him, that he always wants what's best for me."

With a sigh, Linda said, "I think he's worried that he's impotent.

"I helped give him a bath to clean him up when we got home from the VA. He smelled terrible; they really had neglected him.

"When I started to undress him, he tried to undress me, but I told him to wait until later after we'd put Mikey to bed. He said it had been such a long time and that he'd missed me so much that he didn't think his body would behave. I told him it was fine if it didn't, but I was sure it would be ready again later.

"But when he was in the bath, and I started to clean his intimate parts, there was no reaction. I chalked it up to Jeff having more self-control than he thought.

"Later that night in bed, when the same thing happened, he pulled away in shame and hasn't touched me since."

Matt thanked Linda for confiding in him and told her he'd guessed as much, then said,

"I don't believe he's impotent for a second. I think he's just depressed, under a lot of pressure, and in pain.

"He's psyched himself out, feels worthless, not worthy of you," then added, "He loves you so much."

Linda agreed that Jeff wasn't impotent, that it was all in his head, and said she loved Jeff just as much. Then she revealed her greatest concern.

"He's being verbally abusive, trying to get me to leave him.

"I don't trust him anymore. I think if I leave him alone for even a day, he'll do something to himself. He's at the end of his rope; I don't think he can stand it much longer."

Matt said, "I'm in California now, but I'm flying to my next duty station in Nevada tonight. I only have a month left on active duty before they have to let me go, but I'm not going to wait that long. Tomorrow, when I report to my new commander, I'll ask him for an early release. If he says no, I'll resign my commission. I promise I'll bc home by the end of the week, even if I have to go AWOL."

Matt paused for a moment, then added, “There’s a psychiatrist that helped Jeff and me back in England. Actually, he and Jeff saved my life: I was so ashamed of what I had revealed to Jeff during one of our flights that I was going to kill myself.

“His name is Doctor Spiegel. He’s working at Brandeis University now, and I will call him after we finish talking and ask for his help. His methods are definitely unconventional, but they’ve always worked. If anyone can save Jeff, it’s him.”

Linda said OK, then asked, “That flight you mentioned. Is it the one when you disobeyed a direct order, pulled off an impossible rescue mission to save Jeff, almost bled to death, and refused the Congressional Medal of Honor?”

Matt sheepishly said yes, but quickly added,

“It’s the same one when Jeff, with a broken arm and probably a concussion, threatened to kill himself unless they used him to give me a direct transfusion, even though he would likely die from shock,” choking up a little with the memory.

Matt regained control and, trying to give Linda some hope, gently said,

"Spiegel figured everything out once; I'm sure he can do it again. We just have to trust him and do whatever he says." Then he asked Linda to contact him again in two days through his dad to give Spiegel time to form a plan.

#

TEMPORARY DUTY ASSIGNMENT TO HANSCOM: 30 JANUARY 1952

Per his orders, Matt reported for duty to USAF Gunnery School Commander Colonel Richard Harding at 0830 on Wednesday, 30 January 1952, at Nellis AFB, Las Vegas, Nevada.

After a short welcome from Colonel Harding, Matt got right to the point. He asked the Colonel for an immediate early release. He said he only had 30 days left to complete his active-duty service and needed to return home to help a friend, another Air Force veteran, that was in serious trouble.

Colonel Harding said he was sorry, but he didn't have the authority to grant Matt an early release. So, Matt asked to resign from his commission instead.

The Colonel was shocked that Matt, a Major and an Ace in both WWII and Korea, was willing to resign his commission for the sake of a month just to help a friend. Then the Colonel thought he remembered something.

"You're that Yetman? You were a P-38 pilot with the 55th Fighter Group at Wormingford. I was with the 20th. We flew P-38s as well and heard about your rescue flight; we were all amazed.

"They told me about your mission in Korea when you pushed another Sabre pilot to safety. That's why you were selected to be an instructor here. We were looking forward to having you with us, if only for a month.

"Forgive me for being a little slow on the uptake; I'm just now connecting the dots. Was the guy you gave the push to in Korea the same guy you rescued in the P-38?" Matt nodded yes.

"I heard that he was injured when he ejected. Is he the friend that needs your help?" Matt nodded yes again.

The Colonel picked up the phone. "Sargent, get me Colonel Rylance at Hanscom."

In a moment, Colonel Rylance answered the phone. Colonel Harding started,

"Hi Mike, it's Rick. I have Major Yetman here in front of me; I think you've heard of him. He's got about a month left before he separates from active duty, but before he does, I'd like to offer him to your new Sabre group as a technical adviser.

"You know about his tour in Korea, right? I think your guys might like a chance to meet him. You can have him free today on a TDY assignment; no paperwork is needed at your end. Only go easy on him. He's got some very important business back there, so be flexible about when and how often he reports for duty."

After the Colonel hung up, he shook a flabbergasted Matt's hand and said, "We don't want to lose someone like you, not for the sake of a month," then added, "Say hello to Jeff for me, and tell him I wish him all the luck in his recovery, though I'm sure with a friend like you, he won't need much."

#

ANOTHER SPIEGEL SPECIAL: 31 JANUARY 1952

Matt arrived home in Swampscott at about 9:00 pm on Thursday. Frank met him at the door and hugged him. It had been over a year and a half since they'd seen each other, and they each noticed how exhausted the other looked.

The dog, Buster, had passed away several months earlier, and Frank was now living alone. It was the middle of winter, and the house had always felt warm and cozy to Matt that time of year. But it now seemed cold and empty. So Matt vowed to do something to brighten Frank's bleak, living-only-for-work life and to get him to retire early. Matt thought, "Time for a new dog," then asked if he could start a fire in the living room's fireplace.

While Matt started a fire, Frank made Matt a sandwich, and then they chatted for a bit before Frank asked Matt about Spiegel's plan to help save Jeff.

Matt had spoken to Spiegel by phone earlier that day while waiting to board the second leg of the Air Force C-54 transport flight from Nellis to Hanscom.

Before devising his plan, Spiegel had called Jeff's Air Force doctors at Travis, who, once he'd described Jeff's deteriorating condition, were very cooperative. They confirmed that Jeff's injuries were confined to his leg and promised to provide Spiegel with unofficial copies of all Jeff's x-rays and medical records.

Spiegel's plan was straightforward and would address each of Jeff's problems, one at a time, starting with the simplest and moving to the more difficult.

The easiest was the financial problem. Matt would go to the bank in the morning and deposit all his savings into Jeff's checking account. Then, Linda would make the rounds tomorrow and pay all the past-due bills, eliminating any financial pressures.

The next problem, according to Spiegel, was that Linda needed to leave Concord. In his view, she'd carried the burden alone long enough, had done all she could, and needed some rest. Also, her presence might be contributing to Jeff's feelings of inadequacy. Things could get rough, and it would be better if she and Mikey weren't there. Linda should trust Matt, try not to think about Jeff for a while, and not visit or call for at least a week.

Matt would borrow Frank's car, drive to Concord, and with no advanced notice, arrive at noon. Linda would tell Jeff in the morning that she had decided to take Mikey to visit her parents in Lowell, MA, for a while and would pack a suitcase, leaving it by the door.

As soon as Matt arrived, while Jeff was still processing Matt's surprise appearance, Linda and Mikey would quickly say goodbye and leave. As soon as they'd left, Matt would tell Jeff he needed a place to stay for a while, giving the excuse that Frank was hosting a visitor from work.

Spiegel believed that exercise had positive psychological effects, so Matt should begin a workout regimen with Jeff, taking him to the YMCA daily to keep his muscles toned and help build his self-esteem.

Matt should cook three meals a day and encourage Jeff to eat. He should try to wean Jeff off the pain meds and alcohol and get him to discuss anything bothering him.

Most importantly, he should keep pressing the need for Jeff to see a private-practice orthopedic surgeon. Spiegel knew a leading specialist in the field working at Massachusetts General Hospital and could quickly arrange a free consultation. Matt should call Spiegel anytime, day or night, if he got Jeff to agree to let Matt drive him to the hospital. It was Jeff's only chance to eliminate his pain.

Finally, Spiegel warned Matt that Jeff might be suicidal, that he'd just been biding his time, waiting for Linda and Mikey to leave. Once they were gone, it was critically important that Matt never leave Jeff's side. Matt needed to be on constant alert to stop Jeff from hurting himself. But to prevent his own burnout, Matt needed to take a half-hour break each night after dinner to go outside and sit in the car alone. He made Matt promise to do this. Then he told Matt that the number one thing to remember was never to trust Jeff.

Matt told Frank he thought Spiegel's plan was a good one and that it might work. But Frank, having been tutored by Spiegel about his methods and knowing how devious and manipulative he could be, recognized something else.

Not sure if he should make Matt aware of what Spiegel's plan was all about, Frank begged Matt to promise to call him if he felt overwhelmed at any point. Then Frank angrily thought, "No matter how this turns out, Doc, I'll never forgive you for what you're about to put Matt through."

Matt seeing the worry on Frank's face, said, "It'll be OK, Dad. I don't know what Spiegel really has up his sleeve, but his plan probably wouldn't work if I did. I trust him, though, and I think you can, too.

"He offered first to provide Jeff with conventional psychoanalysis. But when he said it could take months, I rejected that plan: I couldn't let Jeff suffer in agony that long, and besides, I don't think we have that much time.

"Then Spiegel said we could ask Linda to have Jeff committed to a VA psychiatric hospital, where he'd be safe and couldn't hurt himself, and Mass General's specialist could still treat him.

"But I couldn't let Linda put Jeff in a psychiatric ward; I just couldn't.

"So, I begged Spiegel to come up with one of his specials - an unconventional plan, but something that could work quickly - and he came up with this one.

"I know it's risky, a big gamble, and will probably be physically and emotionally exhausting for Jeff and me, but I think it's worth a try.

"I have some experience with Spiegel, the puppet master. But I'm still willing to go along with his plan and put myself completely in his hands. He's not reckless, and I know he'll take whatever precautions are needed to keep everyone safe."

Then they chatted about lighter things while waiting for Linda's call, arranged by Frank for 10:30 pm.

#

CATATONIC AGAIN: 1 - 4 FEBRUARY 1952

At exactly noon, Matt walked up to the front door of Linda and Jeff's farmhouse and rang the doorbell.

A supposedly astonished Linda answered the door and let Matt in. She hugged him with all her might, with a confusing emotional mix of absolute joy and enormous relief at seeing him and guilt and fear of the plan they were about to put into motion. Until Linda had surreptitiously begun making phone calls to Matt, she'd never deceived Jeff. Now she worried she was becoming an expert at it.

Matt was shaking, but when he saw a shocked Jeff sitting on the couch, with Mikey at Jeff's feet staring up at Matt, he temporarily ignored his reason for being there and rushed them both.

Jeff, forgetting about his bad leg, rose to greet Matt but was instantly reminded of his injury by the sudden stabbing pain in his leg. Halfway to Jeff, Matt saw Jeff grimace and froze.

Awkwardly, not wanting to cause him more pain, Matt slowly approached Jeff, then wrapped his arms around him in a bear hug and leaned backward slightly, lifting Jeff off his feet. Mikey, not remembering Matt but glad for the company and thinking he now had another dad, wrapped his arms around Matt's leg. Then Linda joined the embrace.

After a few moments, Matt began to worry about how to disentangle everyone without hurting Jeff and asked Linda to direct the process. When she had separated and pulled Mikey away, Matt said,

"You're next big guy. Where do you want me to set you down?"

Jeff said, a little defensively, "I can get around on my crutches pretty well and can hop on one leg. I just got excited when I saw you and tried to stand up normally," signaling for Matt to lower him to his good leg. Then he grabbed his crutches to support himself.

Linda took that as her cue to leave. She told Matt she wished she could stay, but she and Mikey were due at her parents' home in Lowell in an hour. She'd be gone for a few days but was looking forward to catching up when she got back.

Matt said no worries and apologized for springing himself on them like that; it wasn't fair.

Linda said, "You're family, no worries. I'm glad I at least got to see you for a few minutes. I nearly missed you."

Then she hugged him again and, trying not to cry, whispered in his ear, "I'm so glad you're here; you have no idea. He's fading fast. I wish I could stay to help."

Matt whispered back, “You are helping; we just don’t know how. We’re both pawns now in Spiegel’s master plan.”

Linda separated from Matt, then kissed Jeff goodbye. She lifted Mikey to carry him to the car and grabbed the small suitcase by the door. Then she and Mikey waved goodbye and left Matt and Jeff to themselves.

Jeff settled back onto the couch, and Matt sat next to him. They were both smiling, glad to be near each other again.

Jeff asked Matt about his service status, and Matt told him he was still on active duty but had lucked out and was assigned to a cushy job at Hanscom for his last month.

Matt asked if he could stay for a few days; his dad was hosting a visitor from work. Jeff said sure but seemed less than enthused to Matt.

Then Jeff brightened and remembered, “I owe you a beer,” and was about to get up when Matt stopped him and said, “I’ll get it,” and went to the kitchen.

When he returned, he handed Jeff an opened bottle of beer, clanged their bottles together, then sat and took a swig from his own.

They started to relax, and Matt again forgot his purpose for being there; he couldn't help himself; he'd missed Jeff so much. So, instead of following Spiegel's plan, they started joking and telling stories while drinking more beer.

By their third beer, they started talking about their last flight together. They both began to choke up a little until Matt mentioned punching Major Dodd. Jeff was amazed and proud of Matt, then they both cracked up and couldn't stop laughing. But when Matt, still laughing, said, "It was worth it, even though he cracked three of my ribs," Jeff stopped laughing and was now deeply concerned. He grabbed Matt's shoulder.

Matt instantly tried to put Jeff's mind at ease. "It was no big deal. I'm fine; everything healed in a couple of weeks. No infection or anything."

Jeff, still not satisfied, put his hand on Matt's chest and tried to feel his ribs to see if they were all right.

Matt said, "I'm fine, really." Then, when Jeff's expression said he still didn't believe him, Matt took his shirt and undershirt off and showed him.

"See. There's nothing there. No bruising or scars. Nothing."

When Jeff touched Matt's bare skin to be sure, he was finally convinced. He hugged Matt in relief, but then, while still holding Matt, he started sobbing.

Matt could only remember seeing Jeff like this once before when he'd found Jeff with his head on Matt's chest as Matt was coming out of a coma. So Matt did what he'd done then: he put his hand on the back of Jeff's head to try to comfort him. Then, in a quaking voice, Matt said, "I promise everything will be all right," and gently rocked them both back and forth.

Matt got up from the couch and moved to Jeff's head. He asked Jeff if it was comfortable for him to lie prone on the sofa.

Jeff nodded yes, and Matt asked if he could raise his legs for him. Again, Jeff nodded yes, and Matt first raised and placed Jeff's good leg, then his injured leg, onto the couch.

With Jeff's head resting on a pillow, Matt covered him with a blanket, then sat on the floor beside Jeff's head, with his back up against the couch. He turned and kissed Jeff on the cheek and stroked his hair, then took one of Jeff's hands and held it in his own, with their fingers intertwined.

In an instant, Jeff was asleep. With tears pouring down his face, Matt thought,

"Oh, dear God, please help him."

Matt spent the next three hours while Jeff slept, berating himself for not being stronger and sticking to Spiegel's plan. He needed to steel himself, follow the plan, and get Jeff to the hospital as quickly as possible. Keeping things as they were and waiting for the VA to get its act together was not an option.

Jeff awoke refreshed but in pain; it had been several hours since he'd taken a pain pill.

When he saw Matt sitting on the floor beside him, he remembered his breakdown and felt ashamed. He'd had a brief moment of joy seeing Matt again, but the pain was relentless, and he'd long since given up on the VA. He had a plan of his own and was determined to go through with it. Matt was delaying him from implementing his plan, so he would have to get Matt to leave soon: Linda could come back any day.

They were both now on the collision course Spiegel had set for them.

Seeing Jeff awake, Matt said, "I'm hungry. What do you want me to make us for dinner?"

Jeff said, "Nothing for me, but help yourself to whatever's out there. I don't think there's much. Linda usually goes food shopping on Saturday," then added as he reached for the bottle of pain pills, "I could use a glass of water, though, while you're up."

Matt brought Jeff a glass of water, then read the prescription from a distance when Jeff put the bottle back down on the end table, which called for two tablets a day, one every 12 hours, taken after a meal.

Ignoring Jeff's instruction not to make him dinner, Matt made spaghetti dinner for two. When Jeff refused to eat with him, Matt, not wanting to fail so soon, pressed Jeff to try and eat a little, creating the first of many conflicts, all following the same pattern.

Jeff got angry, saw that Matt was hurt, then relented but began building resentment.

After dinner, when Matt had returned from his 7:00 pm break outside in the car, Jeff asked Matt to make him a vodka and soda. Matt balked and told Jeff he wasn't supposed to drink alcohol with the pain medicine. So, Jeff made a show of making his own drink.

Around 10:00 pm, only five hours after taking a pain pill and having eaten barely any dinner, Jeff asked for another glass of water. Matt said it was too soon for another pill. So Jeff defiantly got a glass of water himself, then took two pain pills, making sure

Matt saw what he'd done. Then Jeff went to his bedroom to sleep and closed the door without saying goodnight.

Matt tried to get some sleep on the couch, but his mind was too active and wouldn't let him. He tried to think of a way to coax Jeff into following Spiegel's game plan without irritating him. All that occurred to him was a bartering system: he'd trade his help with less risky behavior for Jeff agreeing to do parts of Spiegel's plan.

When Jeff awoke in the morning, he found an exhausted-looking Matt sitting at the kitchen table, trying to cheerfully greet him with a peace offering of a cup of coffee. Jeff felt temporary joy at seeing Matt. But when Matt suggested going to the YMCA for a bit of exercise, Jeff refused. Jeff knew he could barely put a pair of pants on, let alone go to the Y to exercise. What Matt was suggesting was beyond ridiculous. When Matt started making them breakfast, Jeff returned to his room and loudly closed the door, signaling he didn't want to be disturbed.

The day had started badly, but it only got worse. When Matt put the bottle of pain pills on the top of the refrigerator out of Jeff's reach, Jeff exploded. Matt retreated and handed the bottle of pills to Jeff, who shoved them into his pocket for safekeeping. Matt soon lost count of how many pills Jeff was taking, adding to his growing concerns.

Matt made dinner for them both but only left a plate for Jeff, no longer pressuring him to eat. When he'd seen Matt had backed off, Jeff, torn between his love for Matt and a desperate need to end his suffering, tried to please Matt and ate some of what Matt had made for him, even praising Matt's cooking. Then Jeff returned to his room and softly closed his door while Matt went outside to the car again.

Matt's mind was even more uneasy as he lay on the couch, trying to get some sleep. He knew he was losing the battle; it was just a matter of time now. The thought of finding Jeff was too much to bear, though, so Matt resolved to go first.

The third day passed like the first two, with both spending the day separated but no longer eating or speaking to each other.

Matt spent another sleepless night. When Jeff appeared in the morning on Monday, 4 February, he was edgier than ever and was determined to drive Matt away that day.

Jeff started by verbally abusing Matt and then asked when he was going to leave.

Not processing things well, Matt tried to think of a reason why he needed to stay. It had started snowing heavily that night, and the forecast was for the snow to continue for another day. Maybe he could stay until then?

Jeff didn't think he could last that long but figured he'd try to hold on until then. By early evening, though, he knew he couldn't stand it any longer and went to tell Matt he had to leave.

When he looked for Matt, he couldn't find him anywhere in the house. Then he remembered that it was the usual time Matt went outside.

Jeff thought of what he could say to get Matt to leave. Then he knew. He'd call Matt the worst name he could think of: he'd call him a queer.

Feeling overwhelming resentment, Jeff thought to himself,

"Who's he think he is? Coming here and getting into my business, trying to make me feel bad. He has no idea what kind of pain I'm in."

He stormed out the kitchen backdoor on crutches, in just socked feet, forgetting his coat and keys, slamming the door behind him, and accidentally locking himself outside. He thought, "Damn, now I'll have to ask Matt to let me in before he leaves," as he made his way to the car.

On the way, he got even angrier as he saw a strange car parked at the end of his driveway. He'd noticed other cars parked there all weekend. He was in the middle of nowhere and thought, "What's up with that?"

As he approached Matt's car, heavily covered in snow, he couldn't see inside, but he knew Matt was in there from the frosted windows.

He was about to pound on the driver's side window when he heard the worst sound he'd ever heard. He recognized it immediately: it was Matt wailing.

Jeff realized then that Matt had been going out every night to sit alone in the cold to let his grief out. And he now started to piece together all the other clues: of Matt showing up suddenly out of nowhere, of Linda disappearing, and of the strange cars parked at the end of his driveway.

Jeff could only think of one thing: saving Matt. All that mattered was Matt; he didn't care about himself or his pain anymore. Then he thought, "You win, Doctor Spiegel."

Jeff gently tapped on the window. At first, Matt didn't respond; he was too lost in his grief to notice Jeff's tapping. But when Jeff tapped again, Matt rolled the window down.

The sight of Matt pained Jeff as deeply as the pain in his leg. Matt was a mess. His face was drenched in tears, vomit covered the passengers-side of the front seat and his shirt, his hair was soaked with sweat, and mucus was running from his nose.

With all the tenderness he could muster, Jeff asked, “Hey, guy, what are you doing out here?”

Matt could only lamely answer, “Nothing.”

Jeff said, “Well, come inside with me. It’s freezing out here.”

When Matt didn’t move, Jeff said, “I’ve locked myself out. You have to use your key to let me in.”

Matt took a second to process everything, then slowly opened the door to get out.

Jeff stood on one leg, then held his crutches in one hand, placed an arm around Matt, and let him help him to the kitchen door.

Once inside, Jeff, still standing on one leg, helped a now almost catatonic Matt off with his coat.

Then, he had Matt sit at the table while he put the kettle on to make some tea and cleaned Matt's face with a wet dish towel.

After they'd warmed up a little, with both seated facing each other at the kitchen table and Jeff's hand on Matt's shoulder, Jeff spoke to Matt.

"Matt, I know what's going on. You don't need to worry about anything anymore. I'll do whatever you ask."

Matt said, "No, he said I couldn't trust you. He's always right."

Jeff asked, "Who said, Matt? Spiegel? Yes, he's always right. But that was before; it's over now. You can trust me now."

Matt, clinging to his last sane thought, said, "I can't. He told me never to trust you."

Jeff was now stuck at a similar impasse as the one created by Doc Garnett back at Wormingford.

"You can trust me, Matt. I'll prove it. Ask me anything you want. I'll tell you the truth. OK?"

A very wary Matt asked, "Are you going to kill yourself."

Jeff said, “I was. But I’m not anymore.”

Then Matt asked, “Do you have a gun?”

Jeff said, “Yes. It’s in the hall closet, in the pocket of my long overcoat.”

Matt immediately got up to check. He found the gun, removed the bullets, then, like a caveman, started pounding the gun on the floor, trying to break it. Failing that, the mechanic in him kicked in, and he got an ice pick from the kitchen drawer and used it to remove the gun’s firing pin. Then he opened the kitchen door and tossed the pin deep into the backyard. Finally, he put the gun in his pants back pocket, the weight causing his pants to sag well past his hips, and sat back down.

Matt asked, “Are you saving up pain pills?”

Jeff said yes, then told Matt everywhere he’d stashed a supply.

Matt got up, collected all the pills, and flushed them down the toilet before Jeff could stop him: Jeff thought they should have saved a couple.

Then Matt collected all the bottles of alcohol in the house, including the beer, and poured them down the kitchen sink's drain.

When Matt returned to sit at the table, Jeff tenderly said, "See, you can trust me now."

Then Jeff asked the big question, "What do you want me to do?"

Desperately trying to keep focused, Matt said, "I want you to see an expert at Mass General."

Jeff said, "I don't have any money."

Matt said, "Yes, you do. But you don't need any money to see him."

Jeff, now full of a thousand questions but sensing Matt probably had at most two more answers left in him, said, "OK. So how do we do this?"

Matt reached into his pocket and pulled out a slip of paper. Unable to speak anymore, he handed it to Jeff.

Jeff called the number and recognized the voice that answered.

"Hello, Doctor Spiegel, it's Jeff Sullivan. I'm with Matt and ready to go with him."

Spiegel said, "Hello, Jeff. It's very good to hear your voice again. There's a car parked at the end of your driveway, and the driver will take you to the entrance of Mass General. Someone will be waiting for you there with a wheelchair. Linda has already signed all your paperwork. Leave now, come as you are; there's no need to get all dolled up."

Jeff said, "I have no money."

Spiegel said, "There's no charge; you won't need any money," then added, "Your surgeon is probably the best in the world, maybe with the exception of the one you had in Japan. I promise, Jeff, things will get a lot better now."

Jeff said, "I just care about Matt. I'll do anything for him; I just want him to get better. We've done a number on him. He's standing next to me and is practically catatonic. I can't stand to see him like this." Then Jeff moved behind a totally compliant Matt, gently removed the gun from his pants pocket, then threw it in the trash.

Spiegel said, “I know. I’m sorry. I wish I could have thought of another way. But it’s the same prescription with you two. If you let Matt help you, he will get better. I gambled that you would.

“Just so you know, I was scared stiff until you called, but I shouldn’t have been: it’s always been a safe bet to bet on you.”

#

SURGERY AND AQUA THERAPY: 4 – 5 FEBRUARY 1952

When they arrived at the hospital, Jeff was wheeled to the outpatient surgery suite, with Matt alongside. There they were met by the orthopedic surgeon, who’d been called back in from home.

The doctor had received all of Jeff’s x-rays and medical records. He explained to Jeff that the surgeon in Japan had used a lot of metal screws and plates to align and stabilize his shattered bones. Some of that hardware could remain, but some were only meant to be temporary and restricted motion and needed to be removed before any physical exercise was attempted.

Jeff's bones had mended, and the temporary scaffolding restricting motion and causing pain could now be removed. The doctor had identified what he thought was the chief cause of the pain and would remove that hardware first, reopening the original incision.

Removing the hardware would leave holes in the bones, weakening them where screws were removed. So, to eliminate the risk of rebreaking the bones, the doctor would limit the number of screws he removed in any one operation and wait for the bones to naturally fill in before removing any others.

The first operation would require the largest incision, but the follow-on operations would require much smaller, less than ¼ inch-long incisions. In addition, the procedures were considered minor and could be performed on an outpatient basis, so they didn't require admission.

While the doctor explained all this, the nurses started preparing Jeff for surgery. They tried putting Matt in a room with a bed to rest, but he kept wandering back, so the doctor said it would probably be easier just to leave him there as long as he didn't get in the way.

They rolled Jeff into the operating room, then administered a local anesthetic to his leg, letting a still silent but obviously anxious Matt watch through the window in the operating room's door.

The operation went well and only lasted 30 minutes. They rolled Jeff into a recovery room, moved him to a bed, laid Matt on another, and then pushed the two beds together.

Jeff reached over and took Matt's hand, and once Matt sensed his vigil had ended, he fell fast asleep.

The doctor returned a few minutes later and asked Jeff how he was doing. When Jeff said he was fine, the doctor asked Jeff to roll his right foot from side to side.

Jeff, fearing he'd experience excruciating pain if he did, was reluctant but finally complied.

Jeff was shocked that there was no pain. Then the doctor asked him to lift his leg. Again, when there was no stabbing pain, Jeff was stunned and said, "It couldn't have gotten better that fast. Maybe the local anesthesia hasn't worn off yet."

But the doctor said the anesthesia had worn off 15 minutes earlier and pinched Jeff's calve to prove it. Then he asked Jeff to raise his leg and bend his knee. When there still was no pain, Jeff started to weep.

As gently as he could, the doctor said, "Jeff, it will only get better from here. By the time we're done, I don't think you'll have any pain at all, and you'll have no decrease in mobility. And I'm talking a few months for full recovery, not years."

Jeff asked, "Why are you doing this for free?"

The doctor said Mass General was a teaching hospital, and Jeff's reconstruction surgery was the finest example he'd ever seen. He was hoping he could use Jeff as the best example of the state-of-the-art for his students.

Jeff said he could and would be happy to help but asked again, "Why are you really doing this?"

The doctor looked at Matt, then back at Jeff, and then back at Matt before deciding to give Jeff an honest answer.

"My son was a navigator on a B-17 during WWII. He saw a lot of his friends, other crew members, die. Doctor Spiegel is treating him for a form of combat fatigue they now call Gross Stress Reaction."

Pointing at Matt, he said, "My son was on the crippled B-17 Matt saved. He had a closeup view through the plexiglass nose of Matt ramming the German plane. Spiegel said the image of that would have haunted my son forever if Matt had died and would have made his condition much worse. You rescued Matt," the doctor said, pausing to gain his composure, "and so you both saved my son's life. I am eternally grateful."

Still holding Matt's hand, Jeff said, "Matt's pretty modest. He wouldn't like a lot of fuss made. But if you think it would help your son, I'm sure Matt would be glad to meet with him.

"Sometimes holding Matt, knowing he's really safe, is the only thing that helps me cope. For a cause like your son's, I think we can coax a few good hugs from Matt, but you need to warn your son Matt's blushing is something to behold." Then the doctor, feeling a sudden need to touch Matt himself, reached over and gently petted the top of Matt's head.

The young driver, a student of Spiegel's, had waited seven hours to bring Matt and Jeff back to Concord. Matt slept most of their time at the hospital and for the whole drive back. He was still asleep when they arrived home, so the student carried him into the house, placing him on Jeff's bed.

Jeff tried to thank the driver, but he said it was a privilege and the least he could do for two WWII and Korean War heroes.

When Matt woke up at noon the next day, he found Jeff lying beside him, stroking his hair.

Jeff had been up since 7:00 am and spent the morning just staring at and petting Matt. He'd called Frank and Linda the night before to let them know everything was fine and not to worry. But he told them he wanted to spend more time alone with Matt to be sure that he was all right.

Jeff, not knowing if Matt could speak yet, said, "Good morning, sunshine. How are you doing?"

Matt felt refreshed and fully alert. He wasn't sure how much of what he remembered was real or a dream, so he asked Jeff, "Did we go to the hospital last night? Is your leg any better?"

Jeff answered by lifting his leg, playfully wiggling his toes, then kissed Matt, saying, "Yes, to both questions."

Jeff said, "You look hungry to me. Relax, I'm cooking."

Then he got up and grabbed his crutches, saying, "These are just for support. I'm not supposed to put a lot of weight on my leg until some screw holes in my bones fill in. That's why you're taking me to the Y after breakfast for some aqua therapy."

Matt smiled and said, "Do we even know what that is?"

Jeff said, "It sounds like grab ass in the pool. We're good at that."

When they returned from the Y around 5:00 pm, they started preparing dinner together.

They bantered back and forth and were goofing around when the phone rang.

When Jeff answered, the call was from someone he didn't know.

"Hello, Jeff Sullivan? This is Dave Garlow at Raytheon's Missile Systems Division in Bedford, MA. You were recommended to me by Colonel Rylance here at Hanscom. You probably know we make air-to-air and air-to-ground missile systems for the Air Force.

"From your aeronautical engineering background at MIT and your war experience in England and Korea, we think you'd make a great Systems Engineer with us and would like to offer you a position. Are you looking for a new opportunity by any chance?"

Shocked, Jeff said he was and asked how he could arrange for an interview.

Garlow said, "There's no interview required. We're hiring you based on the strength of two recommendations: you couldn't have finer recommendations than these.

"We understand you have a small medical issue, a broken leg, and won't be available to join us until September, but as it turns out, that's good timing for us."

Jeff said, "I only know of Colonel Rylance; we've never met."

Then Garlow said, "Well, to be honest. Rylance is a secondary recommendation. Your primary recommendation came from someone you worked for in the Eighth Air Force."

Jeff asked, "Did it come from Colonel Crowell, our Group commander?"

Garlow said, "No, someone quite a bit higher up than that. You were recommended by another MIT graduate, the former Commander of the Eighth Air Force, General James Doolittle."

Jeff couldn't believe it but quickly accepted the offer. He thanked Garlow and ended the call quickly before Garlow had a chance to change his mind.

When he told Matt, they both went crazy, celebrating, laughing, and hugging each other. They were so excited they could hardly eat dinner.

After they'd finally managed to calm down a little, Jeff remembered a question he had for Matt.

"You said I had money. Where did I get the money from? I'm broke; they're about to repossess my car and foreclose on the farm."

Matt didn't want to answer. All the news was good, and he didn't want to bring Jeff down.

So, Jeff answered for him. "You gave me the money, didn't you, the money you were saving to buy a house?"

Matt looked away from Jeff and said, "I don't care about buying a house."

Smiling, Jeff said, "Well, it's too late for that now; you own half of this one. You should have thought of that before. I hope you like farming."

Things had settled down, and they were relaxing, sitting side-by-side on the couch, when Jeff said, "I think Linda will still want to leave me."

Matt said, "That's crazy. She loves you so much. Where did you get that idea?"

Jeff said, "She wants a baby girl. They always give you a complete physiological exam after you eject, and my sperm count is very low, so I'm impotent."

Matt said, "You're confusing the two. Low sperm count isn't the same as impotent; they're two totally different things. And low sperm count is normal after ejecting. You need to get rechecked; I bet yours is already back to normal for you, which is probably twice as high as average."

Jeff said, "I tried with Linda when I got back, and it didn't work. So I know I'm impotent."

Matt sat for a minute, then said, “You’re always saying I have a magic touch; well, let’s see,” as he closed the gap between him and Jeff.

As Matt unbuckled Jeff’s belt, Jeff said, “No, stop! Why are you trying to shame me?”

Matt said, “I don’t care if you’re impotent or not. That’s not my favorite part of you. I don’t think Linda cares about it, either.”

Jeff, holding both of Matt’s hands, preventing him from undressing him further, said, “Well, it matters to me. She deserves better.”

Matt said, “OK, we’ll make a bargain; you like those. If I can’t get a rise out of you, I get to keep you all to myself. But if Mount Vesuvius over there erupts, you try again with Linda, now that you’re not in agony anymore or have a million other pressures on you.”

When Jeff continued to hold Matt’s hands back, Matt said, “Please, Jeff, let me try,” then gently pulled one of his hands free and unbuckled his own belt, saying, “Here, we’ll keep things even; you can humiliate me at the same time.” Then he turned off the end-table lamp, the only light in the room.

Jeff released Matt’s other hand and allowed him to resume undressing him while he started undressing Matt.

Matt paused to let Jeff catch up, then proceeded slowly, never testing Jeff’s state of arousal by touch.

When they were both down to their underwear, Matt started nuzzling Jeff’s neck but still avoided making any hand contact with Jeff’s groin.

Jeff started to get really turned on by the touch of Matt’s body and groaned when he put his hand down Matt’s underwear.

But Matt didn’t follow suit. Instead, he let Jeff strip him bare and touch him everywhere, including grabbing Matt’s butt.

Jeff was panting now and full of lust for Matt. Just the sight and smell of him was driving him wild. Matt, though, was focused on one thing: getting Jeff’s underwear off without him noticing.

Jeff was kissing Matt on the mouth and all over. And to Matt, Jeff seemed to have a dozen hands caressing him.

Matt had managed to lower Jeff's underwear without Jeff noticing, and Jeff, hungry now for body contact with Matt, started thrusting himself on Matt while writhing and moaning.

It was all too much and over too soon. Matt felt Jeff press against him, discovered his state of arousal, and knew what was about to happen. So, Matt pushed Jeff over the edge by kissing him on the lips and rubbing himself into him.

Jeff exploded first, quickly followed by Matt.

They were both soaked, with almost two years of pent-up lust now covering their bellies, chests, arms, and necks. And Matt's hands had never come close to touching Jeff's groin.

After taking a few moments to catch his breath, Matt jokingly said, "Yeah, it's official. You're definitely impotent."

Jeff said, "It wasn't me; it was your magic touch. I'd never be able to do that with Linda."

Smiling, Matt said, “Oh, really? You know my hands never touched your penis, right?” Then he added, “So, who’s going to give Linda the bad news she’s stuck with you?”

THE END

Thank you for taking the time to read “Sabre Wingman.” Please take a moment to rate and review the book; your interest and feedback are greatly appreciated.

The story continues with “Forever Wingman,” book #4 in the Wingman series, available on Amazon at

https://www.amazon.com/dp/B0BZ637M26

www.ingramcontent.com/pod-product-compliance
Lightning Source LLC
La Vergne TN
LVHW020411121224
798954LV00028B/438
9798363950247